JUNIOR GREAT BOOKS

SERIES 4

SECOND SEMESTER

◆　◆　◆

AN INTERPRETIVE READING, WRITING,

AND DISCUSSION CURRICULUM

JUNIOR GREAT BOOKS

SERIES 4   SECOND SEMESTER

THE GREAT BOOKS FOUNDATION

A nonprofit educational corporation

First Printing

9   8

Printed in the United States of America

Published and distributed by

THE GREAT BOOKS FOUNDATION
A nonprofit educational corporation

35 East Wacker Drive, Suite 2300

Chicago, IL 60601-2298

CONTENTS

8   THUNDER, ELEPHANT, AND DOROBO

African folktale as told by Humphrey Harman

18   THE MAN WITH THE WEN

Japanese folktale as told by Idries Shah

28   ALI BABA AND THE FORTY THIEVES

(from THE ARABIAN NIGHTS)

78   THE GOLDFISH

Eleanor Farjeon

88   BEAUTY AND THE BEAST
Madame de Villeneuve

116   PROT AND KROT
Polish folktale as told by
Agnes Szudek

132   THE HEMULEN WHO LOVED SILENCE
Tove Jansson

154   THE DEVOTED FRIEND
Oscar Wilde

174 THE DANCING
PRINCESSES
Walter de la Mare

190 ALLAH WILL PROVIDE
*North African folktale as told
by Robert Gilstrap and
Irene Estabrook*

198 MR. TOAD
(from THE WIND IN THE WILLOWS)
Kenneth Grahame

221 THE FURTHER ADVENTURES
OF TOAD
(from THE WIND IN THE WILLOWS)
Kenneth Grahame

Dorobo stirred and shivered in his sleep.

THUNDER, ELEPHANT, AND DOROBO

African folktale
as told by Humphrey Harman

The people of Africa say that if you go to the end of a tree (they mean the top) you find more branches than a man can count, but if you go to the beginning (they mean the bottom) you just find two or three, and that is much easier. Nowadays, they say, we are at the end, and there are so many people and so many things that a man doesn't know where to turn for the clutter the world is in, but that in the beginning things were simpler, and fewer, and a man could see between them. For in the beginning there was only the Earth, and on the Earth were just three important things.

The Earth was much as it is now except that there was nothing on it which had been *made*. Only the things that *grow*. If you go into a corner of a forest very early on a warm misty morning then you might get some idea of what the world was like then. Everything

9

very still and vague round the edges, just growing, quietly.

And in this kind of world were three important things.

First there was Elephant. He was very shiny and black because it was a rather wet world, and he lived in the forest where it is always wet. The mist collected on his cold white tusks and dripped slowly off the tips. Sometimes he trampled slowly through the forest, finding leaves and bark and elephant-grass and wild figs and wild olives to eat, and sometimes he stood, very tall, very secret, just thinking and listening to the deep, dignified noises in his stomach. When he flapped his great ears it was a gesture, no more. There were no flies.

Then there was Thunder. He was much bigger than Elephant. He was black also, but not a shiny black like Elephant. Sometimes there were streaks of white about him, the kind of white that you get on the belly of a fish. And he had no *shape*. Or, rather, one moment he had one shape, and the next another shape. He was always collecting himself in and spreading himself out like a huge jellyfish. And he didn't walk, he rolled along. He was noisy. Sometimes his voice was very far away, and then it was not so much a sound as a shaking, which Elephant could feel coming up from the ground. It made the drops of mist fall off the leaves and patter on his broad back. But sometimes, when Thunder was in his tight shape, his voice cracked high and angrily, and then Elephant would start and snort and wheel away deeper into the forest. Not because he was frightened, but because it hurt his ears.

And last there was Dorobo.

Dorobo is a man, and if you want to see Dorobo you have to go to Africa, because he lives there still. Even then you won't see him very often because he keeps on the edges of places, and most people like to stay in the middle. He lives where the gardens fade out and the forests begin; he lives where the plains stop and the mountains begin, where the grass dries up and the deserts take over. If you want to see him you had better come quickly, because as more and more things are made there is less and less room for Dorobo. He likes to keep himself to himself, and he's almost over the edge.

He is a small man but very stocky. He is the kind of brown that is almost yellow, and he borrows other people's languages to save himself the bother of making up one of his own. He is always looking steadily for small things that are good at hiding, and because of this the skin round his eyes is crinkled. He makes fire by twirling a pointed stick between the palms of his hands, and then he bends his face sideways and just breathes on a pinch of dried leaf powder and it burns. Fire is about the only thing he does make.

He is very simple and wise, and he was wise then too, when the world was beginning, and he shared it with Elephant and Thunder.

11

Now these three things were young and new in those days, not quite certain of themselves and rather suspicious of the others because they very seldom met. There was so much room.

One day Thunder came to see Elephant, and after he had rumbled and swelled he settled into the shape that soothed him most, and said, "It's about Dorobo."

Elephant shifted his weight delicately from one foot to the other and said nothing. His ears flapped encouragingly.

"This Dorobo," went on Thunder, "is a strange creature. In fact, so strange that . . . I am leaving the Earth, because I am afraid of him."

Elephant stopped rocking and gurgled with surprise.

"Why?" he asked. "He seems harmless enough to me."

"Listen, Elephant," said Thunder. "When you are sleeping and you get uncomfortable, and need to turn upon your other side, what do you do?"

Elephant pondered this. "I stand up," he said at last. "I stand up, and then I lie down again on my other side."

"Well, Dorobo doesn't," said Thunder. "I know. I've watched him. He rolls over without waking up. It's ugly and very strange, and it makes me uncomfortable. The sky, I think, will be a safer home for me."

And Thunder went there. He went straight up, and he's been there ever since. Elephant heard his grumbling die away, and he sucked in his cheeks with astonishment. Then he went to find Dorobo.

It took him three days, but he found him at last, asleep beneath a thorn tree with the grass curled beneath him, like the form of a hare. Elephant rolled slowly forward until he stood right over the sleeping man, and Dorobo lay in his gigantic shadow. Elephant watched him and pondered over all that Thunder had said.

Presently Dorobo stirred and shivered in his sleep. Then he sighed and then he rolled over and curled himself tighter. It was precisely as Thunder had described.

Elephant had never noticed it before. It was strange indeed, but not, he thought, dangerous.

Dorobo opened his eyes and stared up at Elephant and smiled.

"You are clever, Elephant," he said. "I didn't hear you come. You move so silently."

Elephant said nothing.

Dorobo sat up and put his arms round his knees.

"I'm glad you came," he went on. "I've been wanting to speak to you. Do you know Thunder has left us?"

"I had heard that he had gone," replied Elephant.

"Yes," said Dorobo, "I heard him yesterday in the sky. I'm glad and grateful that he's gone, for, to tell you the truth, I was afraid of Thunder. So big, so loud; and you never knew where he might bob up next. Or in what shape. I like things definite."

"He *was* noisy," said Elephant.

"Now you, Elephant, you're quite different. So quiet and kind. Just think, Elephant, now in the whole world there is just you and me, and we shall get on well together because we understand each other."

Then Elephant laughed. He didn't mean to. It rumbled up inside him and took him by surprise. He threw up his trunk and trumpeted. "This ridiculous little creature!"

Then he was ashamed of his bad manners, and he wheeled ponderously and smashed off into the forest, shaking his great head, shaken by enormous bellows of laughter.

"Yes," he shouted back over his shoulder, "we understand . . . ha, ha! . . . understand one another . . . very . . . well!"

He was a good-natured animal, and he didn't want Dorobo to see that he was laughing at him.

But Dorobo had seen, and although the smile stayed on his face, his eyes were very cold and hard and black, like wet pebbles.

Presently he too slipped into the forest, but he walked slowly and looked carefully about him, and after a while he saw the tree he wanted. It was an old white olive tree, a twisted, slow-growing thing, with a very hard, tough wood. Dorobo searched that tree, and after a long time he found a branch that was straight enough and he bent and twisted it until it broke off.

Then he skinned it with his teeth and trimmed it and laid it in the shade to dry. Then he found thin, strong vines hanging from tall trees like rope from a mast, and he tore them down and trailed them behind him to the river. There he soaked them and beat them into cords against the river rocks, and plaited them very tightly together. When his cord was long enough he took his wild olive branch, which was dry now, and strung the first bow. And he bent the bow almost double and let it go, and it sang for him. Next he found straight, stiff sticks, and he made a fire and burned the end of his sticks a little, and rubbed the charred wood off in the sand. This gave them very hard, sharp points.

Taking his bow and his arrows, he ran to the edge of the desert and found the candelabra tree. The candelabra is a strange tree. It has thick, dull green branches which bear no leaves. And the branches stick up in bunches, a little bent, like the fingers of an old man's hand. And when a branch breaks, and it does very easily, it bleeds a white, sticky sap that drips slowly on the sand. You must never shelter beneath a candelabra tree because if the sap drips in your eyes you go blind.

Dorobo broke a branch and dipped his arrows into the thick, milky sap, and twisted them like a spoon in syrup. Then he laid each carefully against a stone to dry.

15

When everything was ready he went in search of Elephant.

Elephant was asleep under a fig tree, but he woke up when he heard Dorobo's footsteps in the undergrowth. There was something in the way Dorobo walked—something secret and unfriendly which Elephant did not like. For the first time in his life he felt afraid. As quickly as he could he got to his feet and made off through the forest. Dorobo grasped his bow and arrows more firmly and began to follow. Elephant trumpeted to the sky for help. But Thunder growled back, "It is useless to ask for help now. I warned you and you did nothing. You can't tell what a man is thinking by what he *says,* you can only tell by what he *does.* It is too late." From that time to this Dorobo has always hunted Elephant, and so have all men that have come after him.

As for Elephant, he has never again laughed at Dorobo, and has kept as far away from him as he can.

"So far from home, and now this downpour."

THE MAN WITH THE WEN

Japanese folktale
as told by Idries Shah

Once long ago, in old Japan, there was a man who spent his days trudging up and down the mountains collecting wood. This he used to burn and to make charcoal, for he was unable to make a living in any other way. This unfortunate fellow thought that the gods were in some way displeased with him, for he had on his left cheek a large and disfiguring swelling: what people call a wen.

He had gone to many doctors, but whatever treatment they had prescribed had never been of any use. In fact, whatever medicine he tried, the wen grew larger and larger day by day. He was so distressed at his appearance that he shunned other people and gradually became more and more miserable. His wife tried to be cheerful about the matter and pretended to be unaware of it—the wen and the depression into which her husband was falling—however, in the end it made her hate him.

Their life as charcoal burners was not one of much happiness, and for all the wood he could gather, there seemed to be very little financial gain. The poor woman was seriously thinking of running away, back to her own village, and leaving him and his monstrous wen forever.

One day, with an uncomfortable bundle of wood on his back in an osier basket, the charcoal burner went slowly up the mountain track, fingering his wen with exploring fingers, positive that it was larger than the day before.

Suddenly the thunder rolled, the lightning flashed, and heavy slanting rain began to fall.

"O Merciful Heaven!" he cried. "So far from home and so little wood, and now this downpour. Where can I shelter?"

Stumbling and falling, half blinded, he was at the end of his strength when his hands touched the bark of a hollow tree. Gratefully, he eased the basket off his thin shoulders and covered the top with his wide hat. He saw that there was enough space for him to creep into the hollow of the ancient tree trunk. There was scarcely a drop of rain on his head and shoulders as he crouched there, and he pulled his thin coat around him, removing his sandals to rest his aching feet. The thunder rolled, and it seemed as if the world was about to crack into millions of pieces. But as quickly as it had begun, the storm ceased. The charcoal burner fingered his wen and was just about to creep out of the tree when he heard the tramp of feet. The rays of the setting sun played on a group of people who came marching along the mountain path, lighting them with a crimson glow.

"Whoever can they be?" wondered the man, quickly retrieving his sandals and slipping his feet into them.

He still remained inside the tree hollow, for the sound of wild piping came to his ears. With staring eyes he gazed at a multitude of creatures; they were the strangest he had ever seen in his life. There must have been about a hundred of them, a troop of what he now realized were some sort of enchanted beings.

They were all of strange shapes; some were tall, covered with creepers, hung with curious beads. Others were small and shrunken like skeletons with phosphorous eyes, dancing disjointedly, yet with gay abandon. Some had the mouths of crocodiles, snapping like castanets, keeping in time to the sound of drums almost martial in their rhythms.

There were elves with one eye in the middle of their foreheads, dwarves with tremendous feet, all stamping and leaping along the mountain path in perfect time with the shrill piping and drumming. There were pale witches with long black hair, and huge, dark giants dressed in bear skins. Those who did not have musical

21

instruments had magic wands in their hands, or claws, or paws; but each was leaping and pirouetting in joy and excitement. Some had two horns, some had only one, but each contributed noisily to the general merriment and air of carnival.

Not daring to show himself, the frightened charcoal burner peeped through a knothole and held his breath. They came to a stop just near his hiding place, and the stamping and music grew louder.

They made a large circle, ambling or hopping, round and round, with one of their number in the middle (the head demon evidently) jumping as high as the others' heads in a series of extraordinary leaps. They lit a huge bonfire and, holding up torches which they ignited there, shouted and sang at the top of their voices.

The firelight gleamed on furry legs, shining tusks, or flashing eyes. As he watched and heard the music, the charcoal burner became as gay as they. Forgotten were his wen and his predicament; he leaped into the firelight, and his feet carried him round in a most lively dance. His wen bobbed about, but he did not even try to cover it as usual with one hand. His arms were flung into the air, and he danced crazily, willing and fey, with all the others enjoying themselves round the fire.

"Well done! Excellent timing!" shouted the head demon. "Keep it up, human being, we are much entertained!" Each demon roared or screeched encouragement. The man danced like one whose very life depended on his feet not touching the ground for more than a split second.

The lesser demons piled more wood on the flames; others carried torches round and round. The laughter and screeching grew in intensity, and so did the intricate dancing of all present.

The charcoal burner managed to hold his own in that mighty throng. He laughed as he had not done since the night of his wedding so many years ago, when he felt himself to be the happiest and most favored man of the village where he was born.

At last, completely worn out, he came to a sudden stop and felt terribly thirsty. As if he had read the charcoal burner's mind, the head demon handed him a bowl of wine. The flavor was amazingly good, and it slipped down his throat like a priceless elixir. He felt as good as ever within a few seconds of having drunk, and he felt the gleaming eyes of the head demon upon him. "You have danced well," said the demon with sincerity. "We have been immensely privileged to have you in our little company. Never have we seen a human who could keep up with our ideas of revelry, let alone surpass us!"

"No, no," said the charcoal burner politely. "It was most remarkably good of you to allow my faltering steps to . . ."

"Faltering steps! You are a master of the dance!" roared the demon, pressing the wine bowl upon the man once more. "I speak for all of my people when I say we

23

have tonight, in fact, learned much in the way of steps from you! You must come tomorrow night and teach us more."

Very flattered by the important demon's attentions, the human being could scarcely believe his ears. "Tomorrow night? O Noble Entity, I would like nothing better in this world. Just let me recover my strength, and I will with all my heart attend your revels here, for I am most amazed by your frivolity," he answered gallantly.

"Just a moment, though," said the head demon, as his minions refilled his wine bowl and lavished every attention on him. "Human beings sometimes find life so demanding that they forget our invitations. Let us see what sort of a pledge you can leave with us so that we can be sure that you will come back."

A few of the demons held a consultation, and when they had made a decision, they came to the head demon and said, "Lord Demon, we have democratically decided that, as some humans consider a wen to be a very fortunate thing to have, we will ask the man to leave that as a sign of his good faith."

"Done," said the head demon. "With your permission, good sir, of course. Just a small prick!"

The charcoal burner's finger went up to his cheek in his usual gesture of dismay. He felt a minute twinge, as if a gnat had stung him, and at that moment the entire devilish company vanished. And, with them, his wen had also disappeared.

He could not believe his good fortune. The moon was now up; all signs of the fire the demons had lit and danced around had gone. He slipped his osier basket onto his back, loaded with the wood he had collected, and made his way home with his mind in a turmoil.

His wife was delighted to see him without the monstrous wen. Her heart was uplifted, and she decided not to run away after all. Life would now be much better, with the hideous lump removed from her husband's face. He told her everything, from start to finish, and her eyes were like a fawn's in the lamplight. All the love she had had for him on their wedding day returned. But more was to come. In the bottom of his osier basket, when the wood was all taken out and stacked in the hut, were a hundred pieces of finest silver money.

"Husband! Husband! You will never have to work again collecting wood. We can enter some other, nice clean business. Let us give thanks to the gods for what they have caused to happen tonight!" cried the woman in the height of excitement.

Now, next morning, the tale was told all round the charcoal burner's circle of friends. One neighbor, a baker, said:

"O dear brother, let me go in your place, please, so that I could have this wen removed from my cheek, for it has plagued me greatly since it appeared a few months ago. If only I could go and meet those demons, the dancing would be quite easy to do, I'm sure, and I certainly could do with a hundred pieces of finest silver to get myself a new oven!" His wife added her screams and tears to his request.

So the kindly charcoal burner told the baker where to go, and the neighbor set off gaily up the mountain track. He reached the hollow tree and settled down for a long wait, eating some salted fish and bread while he looked forward to the devilish train's arrival. He had a large osier basket with him, in which he had hoped to take his silver home. No sooner had the sun disappeared than he heard the tramp of the approaching throng. Pipes, flutes, and drums grew louder and louder. Singing and shouting, the demons came, as before, into the clearing. Their heads tossed; their eyes and teeth gleamed in the starlight. The festivities began, the fire was lit, and the demons started dancing. Soon the whole mountainside was reverberating with sound.

"Has the man not come, as he promised he would?" some of the demons began to ask each other.

"Here I am, just as I agreed!" shouted the baker, running towards them. He took out his fan, and covering his wen, began to dance and sing as hard as he possibly could. But his feet were not as nimble as those of the charcoal burner, and he had no natural rhythm at all. He just seemed to shuffle and hop, with no more grace than a goat. The demons looked on with distaste, and several gave him the thumbs-down sign. The head demon snarled with rage as the man cavorted clumsily round the fire. "Your feet are like lead, nothing like last night's performance!" he roared, and the others screeched insults, spitting at the baker like wildcats. "This won't do; we are not at all amused by this behavior. Where is your heart tonight? Here, take your pledge and go, leave us this instant!" Thunder rolled, lightning flashed, rain fell. The roaring and offensive remarks hurled at him so terrified the baker that he ran for his life, a wen on either cheek.

Hurriedly, Ali Baba drove his donkeys back to town.

ALI BABA AND THE FORTY THIEVES

from The Arabian Nights

Once upon a time there lived in a city of Persia two brothers. One was called Cassim and the other Ali Baba. Their father had died early and had left them only very little property. The brothers had divided it in halves and shared it equally. You would now think that their circumstances were similar. But fate had decided differently.

Cassim married the daughter of a rich merchant. After her father's death she inherited a well-stocked shop and large estates. Cassim had now become one of the richest men in the city. By skillful trading his property kept growing.

Ali Baba, however, had married a poor man's daughter who did not even bring a dowry to the marriage. So his small inheritance was used up quickly. Poverty and deprivation were the couple's daily companions. Ali Baba, his wife, and their only son lived in a miserable hut. He earned his livelihood by selling wood. For this purpose he used to journey to the mountains to fell trees. He then loaded the wood on his three donkeys and brought it down to the town, where he sold it.

One day he had gone to the wood again. He had just felled enough trees for loading the donkeys when he suddenly saw in the distance a cloud of dust which came nearer and nearer. He looked carefully, and when the cloud came closer, it turned out to be a group of riders, who came along on horseback at a fast pace. He saw also that they were wearing sparkling breastplates and shining weapons, and great terror befell him. True, nobody had ever heard of thieves in those parts, but the idea occurred to Ali Baba that they might be thieves all the same, and he was afraid they might murder him, and he wondered how he could save himself. He left the poor donkeys to their fate, climbed up a tall tree, and hid between its branches. In that way he could see everything that was going on without being seen himself. The tree grew at the foot of a sheer rock which was much higher than the tree, and so steep that nobody could climb it.

The riders, all young, tall men, dismounted at the foot of the rock. Ali Baba counted forty. After looking at their faces and their behavior he could not doubt that they were thieves. He was not mistaken; they were indeed thieves, but they did not carry on their trade in those parts. They did their thieving somewhere else. They came to this forest only to hold their regular meetings.

Each of the thieves unsaddled his horse, tied it to a tree, and threw a bagful of oats over its head. They had carried these sacks behind them on horseback. Then they took their saddlebags off, and these appeared to Ali Baba to be very heavy. He supposed they were full of gold and silver.

Now the tallest of the thieves, probably the leader, slung his saddlebag over his shoulder and approached the rock. Right above him in the branches of the tree, Ali Baba was sitting, trembling and looking down. The other thieves were following their captain. He stopped in front of a small door in the rock. It was so completely overgrown with thorny bushes that Ali Baba would never have noticed it. The leader now uttered the strange words:

"Open, Sesame!"

Hardly had he spoken them, when the small door opened. Now the thieves entered the rock. They all walked past the captain, who waited until the last one had gone in; then he followed. Noiselessly the door closed behind them.

For a long time the thieves remained inside. Ali Baba had to remain sitting in his tree and waiting. He was afraid they might come upon him just as he was descending. At last the door opened again. The captain stepped outside and let one after the other of the thieves walk past him. Ali Baba noticed that their saddlebags were now empty. When the last thief had come out, he heard the words:

"Shut, Sesame!"

and the door in the rock closed by itself again. Now each of the men went up to his horse, saddled it, hung his bag over the saddle, and swung himself up. Then they all rode away in the direction from which they had come.

Ali Baba followed them with his eyes until they had disappeared from sight. But still he did not dare descend from his tree. He was afraid one of the thieves might have forgotten something and would come back for it. At last, when everything had remained quiet for some time, he climbed down. He walked through the undergrowth up to the small door and studied it for a long time, thinking: Should I say the words the captain uttered? Ali Baba had kept the words in mind. He pondered about it for a long time, but as he wanted to find out what was behind the door, he eventually uttered the words:

"Open, Sesame!"

At once the door opened wide and Ali Baba could enter. Behind him the rock closed, but he was not worried about that. He knew how to open the door again.

He had expected to find a narrow, dark cave. Instead he saw a large, bright vault. It had been built by human hands and was paved with marble and adorned with high pillars. It received its light through openings in the ceiling. In this hall, everything you could wish for was stored. Large bales of cloth, valuable carpets, gold, brocade, and magnificent clothes were lying in heaps. Ali Baba, however, was especially attracted by the enormous quantity of silver and gold. It was lying about there in ingots and coins, partly heaped up like sand, partly packed in sacks. Numerous pearls and jewels sparkled in all the colors of the rainbow; like pebbles on the beach they were lying round the hall. It seemed to Ali Baba as though this cave had been the thieves' store for centuries.

He did not waste time. He gave no attention to the carpets and the silver. He walked straight to the bags with the gold. Of these he took as many from the cave as his donkeys could carry. Each time he wanted to enter or leave he called out:

"Open, Sesame!"

and the door duly opened. When he had carried out enough, he collected his donkeys. He loaded the sacks on their backs and put a layer of wood on top, so that nobody would notice what was underneath.

Hurriedly, Ali Baba drove his beasts of burden back to town. When he arrived home he pulled them into the yard quickly and locked the gate carefully behind him. Nobody must come upon him unawares! The few pieces of wood he put into the usual place. The sacks of gold, however, he carried into his house for his wife to see. One after another, he placed them in front of her. The woman watched what he was doing with increasing surprise. At last she lifted one of the sacks and felt it. She realized it was filled with gold. Now she grew suspicious and thought her husband had stolen it.

"Husband," she reproached him, "if you have been so wicked . . ."

Ali Baba interrupted her with the words: "Quiet woman, I am not a thief. I did not steal anything. I took this gold from thieves. Enjoy our good fortune and listen to what happened."

And he shook the sacks out. Their contents made a great heap of gold. The woman was dazzled by its splendor. Now Ali Baba told her the story from beginning to end. Finally he impressed on her that she must not breathe a word about it to anybody. By now the woman's terror had changed to pleasure. She was beside herself with joy. She wanted to count the gold piece by piece, but Ali Baba stopped her impatiently.

"You are a fool," he said. "How long do you think it would take you to count it? I will dig a pit and bury the gold. We shall have to be quick; nobody must know of our secret."

"But I would like to know how much it is," said the woman. "I shall run over to our neighbor and borrow a measure. Then I can measure it while you are digging the pit."

"Woman," replied Ali Baba, "you had better leave that be. But I suppose you will not be deterred. All right, do as you like, only do not give our secret away."

In order to borrow a measure, Ali Baba's wife went to her brother-in-law, Cassim. But Cassim was out, so she asked Cassim's wife. The sister-in-law wanted to know if she wished to have a large or a small measure. Ali Baba's wife asked for a small one.

"Willingly," said the sister-in-law. "Just wait a minute. I will bring it along presently."

She went to get the measure, thinking: Those people have nothing. What do they want a measure for? She hit on the idea of sticking some wax on the bottom of the measure, to which some of whatever was to be measured would then stick. When she handed it to her sister-in-law, she apologized for the long time it had taken her to get it and explained she had had to search for it.

Ali Baba's wife thanked her, and ran home unsuspecting. She put the measure on the heap of gold. Then she filled it with the gold and emptied it into the pit again and again, until the lot had been measured. She was very satisfied with the number of measures and reported it to her husband. He had, in the meantime, finished digging the pit; now he carefully heaped earth on the gold, so that nobody would see anything.

The woman, however, returned the measure to her sister-in-law. She had no idea that a gold piece had remained stuck to the outside.

"Sister," she said, "I am returning your measure. You see I have not kept it long. Many thanks for it."

Ali Baba's wife went home happily. Cassim's wife, however, turned the measure upside down and looked at the bottom. To her amazement she saw a piece of gold sticking to the wax. She thought her eyes were deceiving her. Then she examined the coin carefully and realized that it was a genuine gold piece.

"How is this?" she exclaimed. "Since when has Ali Baba got so much money that he has to calculate it by measure? Where did he get the riches from? How did he acquire so much gold?" And the devil of envy arose in her heart.

Cassim, her husband, was still not at home. He was busy in his shop and never returned before nightfall. She could hardly await his arrival. She was burning with impatience to tell him the news. At last he opened the door and entered.

"Cassim," she said to him, "you think you are a rich man! You are mistaken. Your brother Ali Baba is a thousand times richer than you. He does not count his money; he measures it."

In bewilderment Cassim asked her what she meant; so she told him of her ruse. Then she showed him the piece of gold that had remained stuck to the measure. It was very old. The name of the king and the inscription were completely unknown to him.

So Cassim, too, gained the conviction that his brother must be enormously rich. But he was not pleased about it. Envy seized him, and caused him to lie awake all night. His avarice gave him no peace or rest.

The next morning, before daybreak, he betook himself to Ali Baba's house. Since his marriage he had not once paid a call on him. He did not want to count him as a brother. Even now, he did not call him that.

"Ali Baba," he said, "you pretend to be poor and needy. You behave as though you were a beggar. And yet you have so much money that you have to measure it."

"Dear brother," said Ali Baba, "explain yourself. What is the meaning of your words?"

"Do not make believe," replied Cassim, and produced the coin. "Have a look at this gold piece. My wife found it stuck to the bottom of the measure that your wife borrowed from her. How many such pieces do you possess?"

Now Ali Baba realized that his brother and sister-in-law had got to know of the matter which he had wished to keep an utter secret. But his wife's mistake could not be undone, so he swallowed his anger and confessed to his brother that by chance he had discovered a thieves' den. He also told him of the treasures that were stored there. Eventually he suggested to his brother that he would share the treasure fairly with him, but he would have to keep the secret. Since he knew the magic formula, he could always enter the cave.

"What you have told me is not enough," replied Cassim haughtily. "I want to know everything. Where is the treasure? How does one get in? I shall go to the cave myself and take what I please. If you do not tell me the magic formula, I shall lay information against you at court. Then you will even lose what you have already got, and I shall receive a reward for having revealed your guilt."

Ali Baba was not afraid of his brother's threats. But he was a good-natured man and told his brother everything. He indicated exactly where the treasure was. He even told him the magic formula which opened the secret door. That was all Cassim wanted to know; he rose and hurried home. He wanted to get a start on his brother and remove all the treasures for himself.

He at once prepared ten mules, loaded two large boxes on each of them, and got rope and saddlebags ready.

Next morning before daybreak, he started on the journey. He had made up his mind to fill all the boxes.

If he should not be able to get everything into the boxes, he would collect it later. He traveled the route Ali Baba had described to him and reached the rock. He recognized the tree in which his brother had hidden himself. Among the thorny bushes he saw the secret door. Loudly he pronounced the words:

"Open, Sesame!"

Immediately the door opened. Cassim entered the rock. Behind him the door closed.

His surprise grew every minute as he beheld the treasures. There were much greater riches than he had imagined. Dazedly he walked about. He felt and examined the bales of cloth, the gold, the jewels. He would have liked to stay all day and feast his eyes on the sparkle of the precious metals. But then he thought of his mules outside the cave, so he carried sacks full of gold to the entrance so as to have them handy for loading on to his beasts of burden. When he had finished collecting, he wanted to open the door, but the magic formula had escaped him. He called:

"Open, Barley!"

But the door remained shut. In his fright he called the names of other kinds of corn, but the door did not open.

Cassim had never expected anything like that to happen. He put down the sacks and sat on them in despair. Horror took hold of him. He racked his brain to recall the magic formula, but no matter how hard he thought, the word did not come back to him. He rose from his seat and paced up and down the cave. The treasures did not interest him any longer. He wrung his hands and plucked at his beard. His heart was filled with terror. He was afraid he was lost.

But let us leave Cassim bemoaning his fate. He does not deserve our pity.

Let us turn to the thieves. They had just attacked and robbed a caravan and were returning to their cave laden with treasures. By that time it was about midday. When they got near, they saw the mules with the boxes. They rode at them at full speed, and the animals were terrified and ran into the wood. Now the thieves wanted to find the owner of the mules. So they searched round the rock, pushed their way through the shrubs, and looked up all the trees. The captain, however, went to the door of the cave with a few of his comrades and uttered the magic formula.

Cassim in the cave had heard the trampling of hooves and realized that the thieves had returned. In his fear he thought of a way of escape. He stationed himself close by the door; as soon as it opened, he was going to rush out. Then he heard the word "Sesame" that had escaped him, and immediately the door opened wide. Cassim ran out with such speed that he knocked the captain over. He was able even to pass the second thief, but there were too many; he could not escape them all. One of them ran his sword into Cassim's chest, and he fell down dead.

The thieves now cautiously entered the cave; they wanted to make sure that there were no other people hidden inside. They returned the sacks which Cassim had taken to the door to their usual places. That there were several missing, they did not notice. They wondered how Cassim could have entered the cave. They were sure the secret of the door was safe, for he would have had to know the magic formula and nobody but they knew that. They had no idea that Ali Baba had been eavesdropping on them. The dead man could not have entered from the top: the openings in the ceiling were too small and too high up for that, and the rock itself was steep and slippery. Now they began to make their treasure secure. They decided to quarter Cassim's corpse and to hang up two pieces on the right and on the left close inside the door as a deterrent to anybody who might enter the cave. They themselves were going to leave the cave alone for quite a time, at least until the smell of the carrion had abated. Then they mounted their horses and rode away in order to continue their thieving on the busy caravan routes.

In the meantime, Cassim's wife had become very anxious. It was now pitch dark, and her husband had not returned. Full of fear, she ran to Ali Baba.

"Dear brother-in-law," she said, "I am sure you know that your brother has gone into the wood. So far he has not returned. I am terribly worried; I fear he has met with an accident."

Ali Baba had had similar thoughts. Therefore, he had refrained from going into the wood as usual, in order to avoid any cause for a quarrel with his brother. Now he, too, believed that some misadventure had befallen Cassim. But he remained calm and soothed his sister-in-law, saying that Cassim would certainly not return before the dead of night, so as to keep the matter as secret as possible.

This consoled Cassim's wife, and she went home and waited patiently until after midnight. When her husband had still not returned, she became restless again. When morning approached she was deeply worried, and she could not even relieve herself by crying, for the neighbors might have heard her. At daybreak she ran to Ali Baba again, and, sobbing wildly, she told him that her husband had not yet returned.

Now Ali Baba immediately set out with his three donkeys. He rode into the wood to the rock, looking right and left for his brother and seeing no sign of him. But near the entrance to the cave he discovered traces of blood; this seemed to him an ill omen and his heart sank. He walked towards the door and uttered the magic words:

"Open, Sesame!"

The door swung open. With a frightful shock he saw to the right and to the left of the door the bits of his brother's corpse, and he had to get a firm grip on himself not to scream loudly with horror and grief. However, he did not waste time. Despite Cassim's unbrotherly behavior, he had to pay him the honor of the last respects. Among the goods in the cave he found several valuable pieces of cloth. In these he wrapped the parts of the corpse and loaded one of the donkeys with the bundles. On it he put some brushwood so that nobody would see anything suspicious. The other two donkeys he hurriedly loaded with sacks of gold, and covered them, too, with dry wood. Then he ordered the door to shut.

He returned to town. At the edge of the wood he stopped; he did not wish to reach his home until nightfall. When darkness had fallen, he drove the donkeys with the gold to his house and requested his wife to unload them and bury the gold as quickly as possible. In a few words he told her of Cassim's fate. Then he led the third donkey to his sister-in-law's house.

Cautiously Ali Baba knocked at the door. It was noiselessly opened by Morgiana, his brother's maid, an extremely clever girl. When he had unloaded the bundle with the corpse in the yard, he drew Morgiana aside. "Listen to me, Morgiana," he whispered. "What I am going to tell you now you must never divulge to anybody. This bundle contains your master's corpse; he must be buried according to the prescribed rites. It must look as though he has died a natural death. Now take me to your mistress, so that I can report to her. You, however, pay careful attention to what I am going to tell you."

Morgiana informed her mistress of Ali Baba's arrival, and the sister-in-law asked him in at once. She had been waiting for him with impatience. "What sort of news do you bring me?" she asked him. "Your expression bodes no good."

"Sister-in-law," replied Ali Baba, "you must listen to me quietly from beginning to end, and you must never tell anyone a single syllable of our conversation. Promise me that. It is as important for you as it is for me."

She promised everything. Stricken with profound grief she listened to her brother-in-law's report.

"A terrible misfortune has befallen you," he concluded, "but there is nothing we can do. What Allah ordains, we must take upon us. For consolation I have a suggestion: When you have mourned your husband long enough, I shall marry you; then I can join my property with yours. My wife will not be angry or jealous. She is sensible and does as she is told. In that way we can remain one family. We shall be able to live well on our property, for we have now ample money and possessions. But first we must pretend that Cassim died a natural death. Here you can rely on Morgiana. She will find ways and means to arrange everything satisfactorily."

Cassim's widow did not need long to consider Ali Baba's suggestion. In addition to her fortune she was going to have a second husband, and he was richer than she would ever be. Therefore she did not refuse the proposal, and it helped her to get over her first husband's death. So she refrained from the usual loud lament. Ali Baba now knew that she would accept his offer, and he left her house somewhat less worried. Before he went home, however, he instructed Morgiana in the part she was to play.

Morgiana left the house immediately after Ali Baba. She ran all the way to the chemist's shop and arrived there out of breath and very agitated. She ordered a medicine that one gives to people who are dangerously ill. The chemist gave her what she had ordered and asked sympathetically who was ill in her master's house. "Oh," she said, "it is the master himself. He is fatally ill."

With these words, she took the medicine which, of course, could not now be of any use to Cassim, and hurried home.

Next morning, Morgiana turned up at the chemist's shop again. With tears in her eyes she requested the chemist to give her an even stronger medicine, which is given to the sick only when their condition is desperate. "My poor master," she cried, "even this medicine will not help him. What a good master he was! And now I am to lose him!"

People noticed how Ali Baba and his wife kept running to Cassim's house all day with misery on their faces, and so the rumor of his illness quickly spread all over the city. It therefore came as no surprise to them when Cassim's wife and Morgiana broke into loud lament. It simply informed them of the fact that Cassim had died.

Early next morning Morgiana went to see a venerable old cobbler in the market square. He was wont to open his shop long before the other shopkeepers. She bade him good morning especially politely. At the same time she pressed a piece of gold into his hand. The cobbler was a cheerful, witty old fellow, known all over the town as Baba Mustapha. As there was not yet much daylight, he examined the coin carefully and realized that it was gold.

"A fine piece of money!" he exclaimed. "What would you like me to do? I will do anything you want."

"Baba Mustapha," Morgiana said, "take your mending gear and come with me straightaway. I shall lead you. When we arrive near our destination, you will have to let yourself be blindfolded."

"No, no," protested Baba Mustapha, "you are asking something of me which is against my honor and my conscience."

"Heaven forbid," said Morgiana, and pressed another piece of gold into his hand. "I am not asking anything of you that would be wrong. Come along and do not worry."

Now Baba Mustapha gave up his resistance. When they had arrived in the vicinity of Cassim's house, Morgiana blindfolded him. It was only when they had arrived inside her master's room that she took the bandage off. There was the quartered corpse. When the cobbler saw it, he paled. Terror overcame him.

"Dear old man, do not be afraid," said Morgiana soothingly. "Nothing is going to happen to you. All you have to do is to sew the parts of this corpse together. Hurry up with your work. When you have finished, I shall give you another piece of gold."

When Baba Mustapha had finished the job, Morgiana gave him the promised piece of gold. Then she blindfolded him again and conducted him back. On the way, she impressed on him that he must keep strictly silent about the matter. At the point where she had blindfolded him on the way to the house, she took the bandage off again. She stopped and asked him to go home alone from there. She watched him carefully to make sure that he did not follow her to find out where she lived.

Morgiana had prepared hot water, so that Ali Baba could wash his brother and anoint him. With the usual ritual he wrapped him in the shroud. The carpenter brought the coffin as ordered, but the family placed the corpse into it so as not to arouse the carpenter's suspicions. Then they ceremoniously mounted the coffin in the middle of the sitting room. After the lid had been nailed on the coffin, Morgiana went to the mosque to inform them that everything was ready for the funeral.

At once the imam arrived with the other servants of the mosque. Four neighbors took the coffin on their shoulders and carried it along behind the imam. Later, other neighbors took turns in carrying the coffin. The imam murmured prayers all the way. Morgiana and the lamenting women followed; they cried loudly and beat their breasts. Ali Baba and many citizens of the town made up the funeral procession. At last they arrived at the cemetery and buried the dead man. Then people dispersed and went their separate ways.

Cassim's wife had stayed at home. She had raised loud wails of lament. The neighbors' wives joined in, as was the custom, so that the whole district echoed with laments during the funeral. Cassim's miserable way of dying remained a secret from everybody. Nobody, apart from the widow, Ali Baba, his wife, and Morgiana, knew what had really happened.

A little while after the funeral, Ali Baba brought his possessions and his money to the widow's house. He intended to live there in the future with his first wife. At the same time, he also announced his marriage to the widow, as was the custom. Such marriages were not at all unusual, and nobody was surprised about it.

Ali Baba's son had to take charge of Cassim's shop. The boy had just finished his apprenticeship to a merchant and had extremely good references. As soon as he showed himself capable of running the shop well, his father would marry him off to a girl of good standing.

Let us now leave Ali Baba in the enjoyment of his new-found happiness and turn to the forty thieves again. When the appointed time had elapsed, they returned to their hideout in the wood. They were greatly surprised that they could not find Cassim's corpse anywhere. Their surprise turned into anger when they realized that a large number of sacks containing money was missing. They were certain now that the dead man must have had accomplices who knew the secret. This thought disturbed them deeply.

"We are certainly discovered," said the captain. "We shall have to take precautions against our enemies at once, otherwise the treasure that our fathers started to collect will be lost in no time. The thief we found knew the magic formula, but there must be someone else who knows it too. That is proved by the removal of the corpse and the missing sacks of gold. We shall therefore have to kill the second man as well, and this will have to be done as quickly as possible. What do you think, men? Or have any of you any better advice?"

The entire gang approved of the captain's suggestion. They agreed that the thief must be found.

"I expected this reply because of your courage and intelligence," the captain went on. "Now, we shall need a bold clever man. He is to disguise himself as a merchant and go into the nearby city, where he must find out if there is talk about a citizen's strange death recently. Then he will have to ascertain where that man lived, and who his relatives are. That our enemy comes from the city seems fairly certain to me. Our man must, however, be clever and cautious, otherwise he might disclose our hideout. If the messenger should bring an incorrect report, he will be punished by death."

At once one of the thieves volunteered and said: "Let me go to the town and explore the situation. Upon my honor I promise to risk my life. If my mission should fail, I will willingly submit to any punishment."

The captain and all his comrades praised him highly and wished him every success. He disguised himself so well that nobody would have taken him for a thief. At dawn he arrived in the city. He went to the market square where only a single shop was open—that of Baba Mustapha, the cobbler.

Baba Mustapha was already sitting on his cobbler's stool, his awl and leather punch by his side. He was just about to begin his cobbling when the thief entered his shop. He bade the old man a kindly good morning. Then he started to talk.

"Tell me, my good old man," he began, "is it light enough for your work? By this half-light, even a younger person could not see well enough, but at your age your eyes must be weak. I wonder that you can pull the threads through the eye of the needle."

"You seem to be a stranger in this town," replied the cobbler, "or else you would know that despite my age my eyes are very good indeed; that is why everybody wants my services. Only the other day, I had to sew up a corpse, and he was lying in a room which was a great deal darker than this one is. Nevertheless I completed my job to the entire satisfaction of my employer."

The thief pricked his ears. He had met the right person already. But he wanted to know more.

"A corpse?" he asked. "How was that? Why should you have to sew up a corpse? You mean to say, do you not, that you had to mend the shroud?"

"No, no," said the cobbler, "I meant nothing of the sort. But I realize you want to pump me, and you have hit on the wrong man. I will not say another word."

But the thief needed no further proof. He knew he was on the right track, and he had to get more information from that quarter. He therefore drew a piece of gold from his pocket and pressed it into Baba Mustapha's hand.

"I will not pry into your secrets," he said, "but I am very discreet. Perhaps the dead man was one of my relations or friends. In that case it would be my duty to offer my condolences to the sorrowing relatives. I would ask you, therefore, to show me the house where the dead man used to reside."

Baba Mustapha weighed the piece of gold in his palm hesitatingly.

"My good man," he said with regret, "even if I wanted to, I could not comply with your wish. A maid came to collect me; at a certain spot she blindfolded me. That is how she took me to the room where the dead man was lying. It was there that I did my job. Afterwards she conducted me in the same manner back to the same place. From there I went home. So you will see that I cannot tell you anything of value. I just do not know the way to that house."

But the thief began anew: "Surely you will remember part of the way. Please come with me. Take me to the spot where she blindfolded you. I shall do the same there. Then I shall take you round all over the place. Perhaps in that way we shall find the house where you did the job. Now every piece of work merits its reward, so I will give you yet another piece of gold. Come along and do me this favor."

The cobbler took the second coin. He examined it carefully and pocketed it. He chuckled and got up.

"All right," he said to the thief, "we will do as you said. But I cannot promise you that I shall find the place."

They set out immediately. Baba Mustapha did not have to lock up his shop; there were no valuables in there. So they went together to the spot where Morgiana had blindfolded the old man.

"It is here that she put the bandage over my eyes," said Baba Mustapha. "I recognize the spot exactly."

The thief now tied his kerchief over the cobbler's eyes. Then he took him by the hand and let himself be led. The old man first walked straight along the road. Then he turned off to the left and then to the right again. At last they came to a narrow passageway. Here the old man suddenly stopped in front of a small house.

"I did not get any farther before," said Baba Mustapha. "At least that is what I think."

Indeed, he was standing just in front of Cassim's house, but now Ali Baba was living there. Before the thief removed the kerchief from the old man's eyes, he hurriedly took from his pocket a piece of chalk and made a sign on the front door. Then he asked the cobbler whether he knew whose house it was.

"No," said the old man, "this house is too far away from my shop. I do not know the people who live in this district."

The thief now realized that he could get no more information out of the cobbler, so he allowed him to go home. He himself quickly returned to his companions in the wood.

Soon after the thief and Baba Mustapha had gone, Morgiana left the house to go shopping. When she returned, she noticed the chalk mark on the door. She stopped and looked at it in surprise. She was disquieted and thought: What is the meaning of this sign? Of course it is possible that it was made by playing children. On the other hand it is also possible that an enemy of my master has something evil in his mind. So she got a piece of chalk and made the same mark on all the neighbors' doors. Then she went back to her work. Neither to the master nor to the mistress did she breathe a word of the matter.

Meanwhile, the thief had arrived back in the wood. Cheerfully he approached his comrades and immediately reported to the captain about the success of his mission. He praised the good luck that had taken him straightaway to the right person. They were all pleased to hear it. The captain most of all praised his skill and his devotion.

"Comrades," he addressed the members of his gang, "we will take up arms and go to the city at once. But take good care to hide the weapons. It will be best if we go one by one. In town we will meet in the market square. Our scout will lead me to the right house, where I shall make arrangements. I shall tell you of my further plans when we have met in the market square."

They all assented to the captain's orders, and soon they were ready to go. In twos and threes, their weapons concealed under their clothes, they reached the town without causing any sensation. The captain and the scout were the last; they straightaway went to the thoroughfare where Ali Baba's house was situated. When the scout saw a mark on the first door he passed, he thought this was the house. The captain went on a little to avoid making himself conspicuous. When he arrived at the next house, he saw the same mark again; so he asked the scout whether it was this or the previous house. That confused the poor fellow; he did not know what to say. As they proceeded, they noticed that there were the same signs on every house door. Now the captain grew angry.

"You scoundrel," he thundered, "which of these houses did you mark?"

The thief earnestly assured his captain that he had put the chalk mark on one door only. He had no idea who could have put the other marks; but now he was so confused that it was impossible for him to be sure which was the correct door. One house was exactly like the others. He had seen no distinguishing mark on the right one in the morning.

The captain realized that his plan had gone awry. So he went to the market square with his companion to meet the other thieves. He ordered them to return to the wood; the day's journey had been of no avail. He preceded them. The others followed at intervals. In front of the rock cave they gathered again. There the captain explained to them why their plan had failed. Then they sat in judgment on the clumsy scout. Unanimously they condemned him to death. Willingly the scout bent his head, which was chopped off there and then.

Now another of the thieves volunteered to scout. He was sure he could do better than his predecessor. It was most important for the gang to eliminate as soon as possible the man who knew their secret. So the offer was accepted, and he knew that he forfeited his life if the mission should fail.

The thief immediately set out on his way to town. Just like the first scout, he bribed Baba Mustapha. In the same way as his predecessor had done, he got to Ali Baba's house. There he marked the door in an unobtrusive spot, but this time he used red chalk. He was sure he would be able to tell it from the doors with the white signs. But again Morgiana, whose suspicions had now been aroused, saw the mark when she got home from shopping, and again she marked all the neighboring doors with the same red sign.

Cheerfully and contentedly, the thief returned to his comrades in the wood. He boasted that he had marked the house with an unmistakable sign; this time it could not be missed. Thereupon the whole gang went back into town again and collected in the market square. This time they were going to carry out the plan that had misfired on the day before.

The captain and the scout went straight to Ali Baba's street. There they noticed with horror that this time many doors bore red marks; again one could not tell the right house. The captain was seized by a terrible fury, but he had to contain himself, or he would have aroused suspicion in the town. He ordered his men to return to the wood and there explained to them why the mission had again failed. The boastful scout, nevertheless, was beheaded as agreed.

Now the captain had lost two valuable members of his gang and had achieved nothing. He thought: I shall only lose more men if I entrust this task to them. My men are brave and courageous in battle. They are suited to plunderings and bloodshed. But when it comes to fraud and ruses, they are helpless.

So he decided he himself would undertake this difficult job. He, too, approached Baba Mustapha and asked him to lead him to the house in question. But he put no mark on it; rather, he looked at it carefully. He walked past it several times and impressed on his memory what it looked like and where it was situated.

When he had done this, he returned to the wood. There he assembled the gang.

"Comrades," he said, "nothing shall come between us and our revenge now. I know exactly which is the house of the scoundrel who stole from us. On walking back I thought of ways and means to manage the matter so cunningly that nobody will get to know anything of our cave and our treasure, which would be disastrous for us. So listen to my plan; but if any of you can think of a better one, he may let me know. Go to the villages and markets in the vicinity and buy nineteen mules and thirty-eight large leather jars for carrying oil. Fill one of them, and leave the others empty. Then bring everything here. You will creep into the jars but take your weapons. I shall get you all into town unseen. The rest leave to me."

Within a few days everything had been supplied. The empty jars were somewhat tight at their necks, so the captain had them made a little wider. Every man now crept into a jar with his weapons. The captain sewed up the openings, apart from a small gap which was to serve as an air hole. Every man should think that these were real oil jars. The captain also painted their outsides with oil, and that made the deception complete. Then he loaded two jars each on a mule. Towards the evening he traveled to town, disguised as a merchant.

He arrived there about one hour after sunset and went straight to Ali Baba's house with his whole train. He wanted to ask for night quarters there for himself and his mules. He did not have to knock. Ali Baba was sitting comfortably in front of his house, enjoying the cool evening air after dinner. The captain halted his mules. Modestly and courteously he bade the time of day.

"Master," he then said, "I have brought all this oil from afar. Tomorrow I will sell it in the market. But I do not know where I can find accommodation at so late an hour. I do not wish to be a burden to you, but could you possibly give me lodging for the night? I should be most grateful to you. Also, of course, I would pay you well."

True, Ali Baba had seen the captain of the thieves in the wood and had also heard his voice. But he did not recognize him in his disguise as an oil merchant.

"Be welcome," said Ali Baba. "You may spend the night at my house."

He made room for him, and the captain drove his mules into Ali Baba's yard. Ali Baba ordered his slaves to unload the animals and feed and tie them up. He himself went to the kitchen and ordered Morgiana to prepare a good supper for the late guest. Also she was to get a bed ready for him in one of the rooms.

Ali Baba then returned to his guest. When he saw that the stranger had unloaded the mules and was looking for a place to sleep in the yard, he took him by the hand and wanted to lead him into the sitting room. But the thieves' captain refused. He said he did not wish to become a nuisance to his host. The truth was, he wanted to remain near his men. But Ali Baba asked him so politely and pressingly that he did not dare refuse any longer. Then the captain partook of a hearty meal and his host kept him company. At last the guest rose.

"I will now leave you alone," Ali Baba said to him. "If you should require anything, just call. Everything in the house is at your service."

The master of the house went to the kitchen to discuss tomorrow's breakfast for the guest with Morgiana. In the meantime the guest wandered into the yard, pretending he wanted to have a look at his mules in the stable.

Ali Baba instructed the maid to look after the guest well. "Also," he added, "I want to go to the bathhouse tomorrow morning. Get the bath towels out and hand them to Abdullah, the slave, and do not forget to cook a nourishing soup for me. I shall be hungry after the bath."

Then he went to his room and got into bed.

Meanwhile, the captain had left the stable and had given instructions to his men. For this purpose he walked slowly past the jars.

"As soon as you hear small stones fall in the yard," he said in a low voice, "cut the jars with your daggers, creep out, and wait for me. I shall be with you in no time."

After that he returned to the house. Morgiana led him into a well-appointed room. She asked him if he wanted for anything, but the stranger needed nothing, so she left him alone. He extinguished the light and lay down on his bed fully dressed, in order to wait a little longer.

Morgiana did not forget the master's orders. First she got the bath towels out and handed them to Abdullah. Then she went to the kitchen to make preparations for the soup and to light a fire.

While she was working, the light of her lamp grew smaller and smaller, and in the end the lamp went out; the oil in it was finished. She turned to the oil jug to refill the lamp and found that the jug was empty, too. She had no candles either and did not know what to do, because she urgently needed light for her work. So she asked Abdullah.

"Do not worry," said the slave, "there is plenty of oil in the house. The whole yard is full of the oil jars that belong to the strange trader. Help yourself to as much oil as you need; he is sure not to mind. Besides, tomorrow we can pay him the price of the oil."

This seemed reasonable advice to Morgiana, and she thanked Abdullah. He went to bed, and she took her oil jug to the yard for filling. When she approached the first jar she came to, the thief inside thought his captain had come. He was impatient to get out of his narrow confines; it was so uncomfortable, all his bones ached.

"Has the time come?" he asked in a low voice.

Any other woman would have been terrified to death. Morgiana, too, was considerably upset. She had expected to find oil in the jar, not a man. But she got a grip on herself at once. She realized how important it was to keep the matter secret. Without showing her disquiet, she said in a deep man's voice:

"Not yet, but soon."

Then she turned to the next jar, and the same thing happened there. And so she went on, until she came to the last jar. That one did contain oil enough to fill her jug. Swiftly she returned to the kitchen, where she cleaned the lamp and refilled it.

While she was lighting the lamp, she gave the matter anxious thought. So her master's guest was not an oil trader, but a thieves' captain! The thirty-seven thieves within the jars were probably about to commit a

61

despicable crime. Something had to be done about it! She went to the yard with a huge kettle and filled it with the oil out of the last of the jars. She returned to the kitchen with the full kettle and put it on the fire, on which she had laid an extra supply of good, dry wood to obtain a powerful flame. It did not take long for the oil to boil and to bubble. She took the seething oil into the yard and poured enough into every jar to kill the man inside.

This deed was a credit to Morgiana. She had shown a great deal of courage and ingenuity. After having attended to the matter quite noiselessly, she went back to the kitchen. She banked the fire just enough to keep her master's soup simmering, then she extinguished the light, bolted her kitchen door, and sat down by the window. She wanted to observe from that vantage point anything else that might occur.

For a quarter of an hour she sat by the window without anything happening. The thieves' captain had waited until everybody in the house was asleep. Now he went to his window and looked down into the dark yard. Nothing stirred; no light was to be seen anywhere. So he dropped some small stones as the signal they had arranged. Some of the stones even hit the jars, but nothing moved; the men did not emerge from the jars. That puzzled him. He threw stones again and even a third time, but all remained quiet. In great alarm, he ran silently into the yard. When he approached the first jar, the smell of hot oil mixed with a horrible odor assailed his nostrils. The same happened when he neared the second jar. He knew at once that his plan had failed. His intention of murdering Ali Baba and plundering his house had come to nothing. He saw that all his men had lost their lives in the same manner. A great quantity of oil was missing from the last jar; with that oil his men had been killed. In despair he saw his hopes destroyed. Now all he could do was to save his own life as quickly as possible. So he jumped over the wall into the neighbor's garden; from there he fled over the fences and hedges until he reached the open country and ran into the wood.

Morgiana heard no more noise, neither did she see the thieves' captain return, so she felt sure that he had fled through the gardens. The front door had been locked and bolted; he could not have escaped through it. She was satisfied that her action had succeeded and went to bed at peace. She had saved her master and the whole house from a gang of thieves.

Early next morning Ali Baba got up and went to the bath with his slave. He had no idea of the happenings of the past night. Morgiana had told neither him nor Abdullah, so that they should not worry.

When Ali Baba returned from the bath, the sun was already high in the sky. In surprise he saw that the oil jars were still in his yard. He thought the strange trader would have gone to the market long ago. So he asked Morgiana why the man was still in the house.

"My master," said Morgiana, "may Allah protect you and your entire house. You are destined for a long life. Last night Allah's benevolence protected you from certain death. Your enemies, however, have perished miserably. Come with me into the yard and see with your own eyes."

Ali Baba followed the maid into the yard. She pointed to the first jar. "Have a look," she said, "at the oil inside!"

Ali Baba bent down to see better. When he noticed a man inside with a bare dagger he retreated with a scream.

"Do not be afraid," said Morgiana. "The man can do no harm to anybody. He is dead."

"Morgiana," exclaimed Ali Baba, "what is the meaning of this?"

"I shall tell you in a minute," replied Morgiana, "but drop your voice. The neighbors need not know our secret. First take a look at the other jars."

Ali Baba looked into every jar, one by one. In each was a dead, burned man with a dagger in his hand. There were thirty-seven men in all. Only the last jar contained some oil. Ali Baba stopped in confusion. He looked at Morgiana and at the jars. At last he regained enough control over himself to be able to speak.

"But what has become of the strange merchant?" he asked.

"That merchant," replied Morgiana, "is no more a merchant than I am. But come to the house. I would rather tell you the whole story inside. There you can sit down comfortably and strengthen yourself with some meat soup."

Ali Baba betook himself to his room and Morgiana brought him the soup.

"Come, come, tell me," he said impatiently. "Tell me the whole story in all particulars. I can hardly wait."

Morgiana complied, and began:

"My master, last night I got the bath towels out as you had ordered and handed them to Abdullah. Then I began to prepare the soup, but the lamp went out, because the oil had come to an end. I could not find any in the jug either, and there were no candles at all in the house. Then Abdullah drew my attention to the oil jars in the yard. So I took the jug to get some oil from them.

"A voice called from the first jar:

" 'Has the time come?'

"I got a shock, but soon composed myself again. It was clear to me that some evil deed was about to be perpetrated. So I disguised my voice and replied:

" 'Not yet, but soon.'

"Then I went from one jar to another, and from each came the same question, and I gave the same answer. That is how I became aware that there was a man hidden in every single jar except the last. That contained oil; with it I filled my jug. Now I knew that there were thirty-seven thieves in your house, and that they were all waiting for a sign to attack you. So I took a large kettle, filled it with oil, and brought it to the boil; with it I scalded the thieves in the jars. Then I went back to the kitchen, bolted the door, and turned the light off. I sat down by the window to watch what our guest would do next. After a while I heard how he threw little stones on the jars. When nothing stirred, he did it a second and then a third time. Then he sneaked down into the yard and went from one jar to the next. As it was so dark I lost sight of him. I believe he must have fled over the garden wall.

"This is the story," she went on, "that you wanted to know. But I can tell you even more. A few days ago I noticed a white chalk mark on our door. I had no idea what it was for. So I went round the neighborhood and made the same marks on all the other doors in the vicinity. The following day I saw a red mark on our door, so I went round chalking red marks on the other doors. Now think that over. I realized all this was connected with the forty thieves in the wood. Why there were only thirty-eight here is not quite clear to me. Anyway, it proves that the thieves are after your life. There are now only three left, but you must take care. As long as there is only one alive, it is dangerous for you. I shall do what I can to watch over you."

Ali Baba now realized what an enormous service Morgiana had done him.

"You have saved my life," he said in gratitude. "From this hour I give you your freedom, and I will look after you in future as much as I can. I, too, am convinced that these men were the forty thieves. Praised be Allah! Through your hand he has saved me from dire peril. I implore him that he may continue to care for me. Now we first have to dig a trench and throw the corpses of these thieves in. We will do it quietly; nobody must hear anything. Abdullah will help me."

Ali Baba's garden was very long; at the bottom it was bordered by tall, old trees. Here, with the help of his slave, Ali Baba dug a long deep trench. As the ground was soft, the work proceeded smoothly.

Then they pulled the corpses from the jars and threw them into the trench one by one. On them they heaped earth and stamped on it to make it firm. On top they spread some loose soil, so that the ground looked just as it had looked before. The oil jars were hidden in the house. The mules were sold one by one, at different times, in the market. In this way Ali Baba did everything he could to keep the secret of his wealth hidden.

Meanwhile the thieves' captain had arrived at his rocky cave, his heart full of anger and grief. Inside the cave he sat down and mourned the fate of his men. Their lives had ended horribly. Never again would he be able to gather around him such a band of courageous comrades. He decided he would avenge their deaths. And his enemy was not to get the treasures in the cave either! By and by he quieted down. In the end, sleep overcame him.

Next morning he put on an exquisite suit, went to the town, and took a room in a fine hotel. He was sure the events at Ali Baba's house must have become known in the town. So he asked the landlord about recent happenings. The man told him of a number of insignificant events, but nothing of the matter about which the thief expected to hear. He saw from this that Ali Baba must have acted cautiously. He probably did not wish to disclose the origin of his wealth. The thief therefore decided to remove Ali Baba by some secret method.

He bought a horse and rode several times to the cave in the wood. Each time he brought with him bales of fine cloth, suits, carpets, precious jewels. In the town he rented a shop where he stored his goods and began a lively trade. Opposite his shop was the late Cassim's business, which was now run by Ali Baba's son.

The thieves' captain now called himself Cogia Houssain. As a new trader he paid calls on the neighbors, as is the custom, and exchanged polite conversation with them. He was obliging and behaved in a dignified manner, and so he soon gained esteem and repute.

Ali Baba's son sought his acquaintance, and soon these two became firm friends. The boy was intelligent and well-educated. The thief liked to chat with him. Now and then Ali Baba came to see his son, and Cogia Houssain recognized him as the owner of the house where his comrades had lost their lives. Then the youth told him that Ali Baba was his father, and now the thief became even more amiable. He gave him small presents and invited him occasionally for meals.

The young man did not wish to accept so many courtesies without repaying the kindness, but he could not invite the trader to his own place, as it was small and uncomfortable. So he talked it over with his father. Ali Baba was only too pleased to be host to his son's friend.

"My son," he said, "it is Friday tomorrow. On that day all the traders keep their shops closed. Invite your neighbor for a walk through the town. Arrange for the two of you to pass my house on the way back. Then invite him to come in. I will not issue a formal invitation, but I shall instruct Morgiana to prepare a tasty supper."

And so, on Friday afternoon, Ali Baba's son and Cogia Houssain went for a walk together. On their way back, the son arranged that they happened to pass through the street where Ali Baba lived. When they reached the front door the youth stopped.

"This is our house," he said. "Please enter, and do me the honor of having a meal with my father."

Cogia Houssain at first refused the invitation. He made a number of excuses, but the young man asked him more and more urgently to add this one more favor to all the others he had already bestowed on him. True, the thieves' captain had already made up his mind to gain access to Ali Baba's house and kill him, but he went on refusing for a while to keep up the pretense. In the end, a slave opened the door. The young man seized his friend's hand and led him courteously into the house.

Ali Baba welcomed Cogia Houssain with a friendly gesture. He thanked him for the honor of his visit and wished him happiness and well-being.

"I am greatly indebted to you," he said. "You are an experienced man, but you do not think it beneath you to contribute to my son's education."

Houssain answered with a few well-chosen words and then wanted to take his leave. But Ali Baba kept him and asked him to do him the honor of being his guest for supper.

"Sir," replied Cogia Houssain, "I thank you for your kind invitation. But forgive me; I cannot accept. Do not consider this as a slight or an impoliteness. There is a special reason for it. You would understand if you knew."

"May I know the reason?" asked Ali Baba.

The merchant replied: "Yes, I can tell you. I must not eat meat or anything else with salt. That would look odd at table, and I wish to avoid it."

In the Orient, if a man eats salt with another, the other man becomes his friend and brother and must never be harmed by him. This is important to know.

"That is no reason to deprive me of the honor of your visit," was Ali Baba's answer. "There is no salt in my bread. And there will be no salt put into any of the other dishes that will be offered to you. So, please stay. I shall go to the kitchen to give instructions to this effect."

Ali Baba went to the kitchen to tell Morgiana not to add any salt to the meat today. Also she was to prepare some other unsalted dishes. Morgiana, who had already made her preparations, and had just been about to put the finishing touches to the meal, grew annoyed.

"Who is that obstinate fellow?" she asked. "Why does he not want to eat any salt? If I have to get fresh dishes now in a hurry, they will not be very good."

"Do not be angry, Morgiana," begged Ali Baba, "do as I tell you."

Morgiana obeyed reluctantly. She was curious to see the strange man who would not eat any salt. When Abdullah had laid the table, she helped him carry the dishes in. Despite his disguise, she at once recognized the guest as the thieves' captain. She also noticed that he was carrying a dagger hidden under his suit. Aha, she thought, now I can see why this scoundrel will not eat any salt with my master. He wants to murder him. Well, I shall prevent that.

Back in her kitchen, Morgiana wondered how best she could carry out her plan. While the guest was eating with her master, she made her preparations. Just when Abdullah called for the fruit for dessert, she had completed them. She herself carried the fruit in, and placed it on a small table by the side of Ali Baba. On leaving the room, she pulled Abdullah along with her, pretending she was going to leave her master alone with his guest.

Now, thought the thieves' captain, the time has come to kill Ali Baba.

"I shall make use of this favorable opportunity," he said to himself. "I shall make them both drunk, father as well as son. Then I will push the dagger into the old man's heart; the son may live, if he does not hinder me. I, however, shall flee over the garden wall, as I did the other day. Only I shall have to wait just a little longer, until the slave and the maid are having their meal."

Morgiana, however, had seen what was in the scoundrel's evil mind; she did not give him time to carry out the wicked deed. Instead of having her meal, she put on a charming dancing dress, a silver head ornament, and a sparkling belt. A dagger encrusted with diamonds was hanging from the belt. When she had finished dressing, she turned to Abdullah.

"Abdullah," she said, "take your bell-drum. We will go into the dining room to entertain our master and his guest."

The slave fetched the bell-drum, banged on it, and walked into the dining room in front of Morgiana, who followed in his footsteps. She bowed low with natural grace. Then she asked for permission to show her prowess in dancing.

"Come in, Morgiana," Ali Baba called to her. "Let our guest see how well you know this art." And turning to his guest, he said: "You see I have everything in the house; I do not have to get strange dancers. My maid and my slave provide that pleasure for me. I hope you will like it."

Cogia Houssain was annoyed about the delay and secretly cursed the two dancers. Again a favorable opportunity had been missed. But he could not very well refuse, so he said he was pleased to have this unexpected pleasure.

Now Abdullah began to beat his bell-drum and sing a dancing tune. Morgiana danced with incomparable grace that would have done credit to a professional dancer. But the fake merchant had no eyes for the girl's charming movements; he gazed angrily into space. Ali Baba and his son, however, gave the two performers whole-hearted applause.

One dance followed another. The steps became quicker and more complicated. At last Morgiana took the dagger out of her belt. Swinging the sparkling blade in her hand, she whirled round the room in leaps and turns. Now she thrust the dagger forward, now sideways. Now she aimed it at Ali Baba, now at the son, now at the guest. At last she seemed to have lost her breath. She tore the bell-drum from the slave's hand with her left, while she was still holding the dagger in her right. Now she held the concave side of the drum towards Ali Baba, as though she were collecting money.

Ali Baba threw a gold piece into the drum, and so did his son. Cogia Houssain was about to do the same; he had already pulled out his money bag. Just when he was drawing out a coin, Morgiana, with the courage of her resolution, thrust the dagger into his chest. The merchant sank back lifelessly.

Ali Baba and his son shrieked with horror simultaneously.

"Wretched girl," exclaimed Ali Baba, "what have you done? Do you want to ruin me and my family?"

"No, master," replied Morgiana quietly. "I did it to save you. Look what I shall show you."

With these words she opened the false merchant's suit and showed her master the dagger he was carrying.

"Do you realize now," she went on, "who the man was? Just look a little more closely, and you will recognize him as the supposed oil merchant. In reality, of course, he was the captain of the forty thieves. He was always after your life. Now you will understand why he did not want to eat salt with you; that is what made me suspicious straightaway, and I was right, as you can see now."

Deeply moved, Ali Baba embraced the girl. She had now saved his life for the second time.

"Morgiana," he said, "I have given you your freedom. That, however, is not enough to express to you my great gratitude. I promised you more to come. Now is the time to fulfill my promise. I will tell you how I am going to reward you for your loyalty and devotion. I am going to give you in marriage to my dear only son."

And he turned to the young man.

"My dear son," he said, "you heard what I have decided. I hope you will bow to your father's wish. You owe Morgiana no less gratitude than I do. Cogia Houssain sought your friendship only for the purpose of killing me. Perhaps he would have made you, too, a victim of his revenge. Morgiana will always be a credit to our family; to you, however, she will be a support until the end of your days. That is why I shall marry you to her."

The young man had not the slightest objection. Marriage to Morgiana was greatly to his liking.

Then they buried the captain's corpse next to his henchmen. It was done quickly and quietly. It was only many years after that the matter leaked out, and then nobody concerned was alive any longer.

A few days later, Morgiana's wedding to Ali Baba's son was celebrated. There was a splendid, lavish meal, accompanied by song, dance, and the usual festivities. Ali Baba was especially pleased, as all the guests praised Morgiana's virtues, although they had no idea of the real motives underlying the marriage.

The last time Ali Baba had been to the cave was when he had found his brother's corpse. For a long time he refrained from going there again. Only thirty-eight thieves had been accounted for. What had happened to the remaining two, he did not know. He thought they might be lying in wait for him in the cave.

But for more than a year everything was quiet. Now Ali Baba was seized with curiosity. One fine morning he mounted a horse and rode into the wood. When he arrived at the rock cave he looked round cautiously. But he did not see any traces either of humans or of horses. The thorny bushes in front of the secret door had become almost impenetrable. That told him that for a long time nobody had been in the cave. So he tied his horse to a tree, crept through the shrubs to the secret door, and spoke the magic words:

"Open, Sesame!"

At once the door swung open, and he entered. He saw that the goods and treasures had not been touched. So nobody had been in the cave since Cogia Houssain's death! Evidently none of the forty thieves was alive any longer, and Ali Baba was the only person in the world who knew of the treasures. He was the master of the immeasurable wealth in the cave. But he filled only one sack with gold, so as not to overburden his horse, and returned to town, serene and contented.

From that time on, Ali Baba lived in peace. Highly esteemed by all his fellow citizens in the town, he enjoyed his wealth in comfortable serenity. Later, he let his son into the secret of the cave and the magic formula. His son, in turn, confided it to his children. They all disposed wisely and modestly of their fortune, so they were loved by the poor and held in esteem by the rich. And so they spent their lives in happiness and joy.

He let the Goldfish dart through his fingers.

THE GOLDFISH

Eleanor Farjeon

There was once a Goldfish who lived in the sea in the days when all fishes lived there. He was perfectly happy and had only one care, and that was to avoid the net that floated about in the water, now here, now there. But all the fish had been warned by King Neptune, their father, to avoid the net, and in those days they did as they were bid. So the Goldfish enjoyed a glorious life, swimming for days and days in the blue and green water: sometimes low down close to the sand and shells and pearls and coral, and the big rocks where the anemones grew like clusters of gay flowers, and the seaweed waved in frills and fans of red and green and yellow; and sometimes he swam high up near the surface of the sea, where the white caps chased each other, and the great waves rose like mountains of glass and tumbled over

79

themselves with a crash. When the Goldfish was as near the top as this, he sometimes saw swimming in the bright blue water far, far above him a great Gold Fish, as golden as himself, but as round as a jellyfish. And at other times, when that distant water was dark blue instead of bright, he saw a Silver Fish such as he had never met under the sea, and she too was often round in shape, though at times, when she seemed to swim sideways through the water, he could see her pointed silver fins. Our Goldfish felt a certain jealousy of the other Gold Fish, but with the Silver Fish he fell in love at sight, and longed to be able to swim up to her. Whenever he tried to do this, something queer happened that made him lose his breath; and with a gasp he sank down into the ocean, so deep that he could see the Silver Fish no longer. Then, hoping she might descend to swim in his own water, he swam for miles and miles in search of her; but he never had the luck to find her.

One night as he was swimming about in very calm water, he saw overhead the motionless shadow of an enormous fish. One great long fin ran under its belly in the water, but all the rest of it was raised above the surface. The Goldfish knew every fish in the sea, but he had never before seen such a fish as this! It was bigger than the Whale, and as black as the ink of the Octopus. He swam all round it, touching it with his inquisitive little nose. At last he asked, "What sort of fish are *you?*"

The big black shadow laughed. "I am not a fish at all, I am a ship."

"What are you doing here if you are not a fish?"

"Just at present I am doing nothing, for I am becalmed. But when the wind blows I shall go on sailing round the world."

"What is the world?"

"All that you see and more."

"Am I in the world, then?" asked the Goldfish.

"Certainly you are."

The Goldfish gave a little jump of delight. "Good news! good news!" he cried.

A passing Porpoise paused to ask, "What are you shouting for?"

"Because I am in the world!"

"Who says so?"

"The Ship-Fish!" said the Goldfish.

"Pooh!" said the Porpoise, "let him prove it!" and passed on.

The Goldfish stopped jumping, because his joy had been damped by doubt. "How can the world be more than I can see?" he asked the Ship. "If I am really in the world I ought to be able to see it *all*—or how can I be sure?"

"You must take my word for it," said the Ship. "A tiny fellow like you can never hope to see more than a scrap of the world. The world has a rim you can never see over; the world has foreign lands full of wonders that you can never look upon; the world is as round as an orange, but you will never see how round the world is."

Then the ship went on to tell of the parts of the world that lay beyond the rim of things, of men and women and children, of flowers and trees, of birds with eyes in their tails—blue, gold, and green—of white and black elephants, and temples hung with tinkling bells. The Goldfish wept with longing because he could never see over the rim of things, because he could not see how round the world was, because he could not behold all at once all the wonders that were in the world.

How the Ship laughed at him! "My little friend," said he, "if you were the Moon yonder, why, if you were the Sun himself, you could only see one half of these things at a time."

"Who is the Moon yonder?" asked the Goldfish.

"Who else but that silver slip of light up in the sky?"

"Is that the sky?" said the Goldfish. "I thought it was another sea. And is that the Moon? I thought she was a Silver Fish. But who then is the Sun?"

"The Sun is the round gold ball that rolls through the sky by day," said the Ship. "They say he is her lover and gives her his light."

"But I will give her the world!" cried the Goldfish. And he leaped with all his tiny might into the air, but he could not reach the Moon and fell gasping into the sea. There he let himself sink like a little gold stone to the bottom of the ocean, where he lay for a week weeping his heart out. For the things the Ship had told him were more than he could understand; but they swelled him with great longings—longings to possess the Silver Moon, to be a mightier fish than the Sun, and to see the whole of the world from top to bottom and from side to side, with all the wonders within and beyond it.

Now it happened that King Neptune, who ruled the land under the waves, was strolling through a grove of white and scarlet coral, when he heard a chuckle that was something between a panting and a puffing; and peering through the branches of the coral-trees he beheld a plump Porpoise bursting its sleek sides with laughter. Not far off lay the Goldfish, swimming in tears.

King Neptune, like a good father, preferred to share in all the joys and sorrows of his children, so he stopped to ask the Porpoise, "What tickles you so?"

"Ho! ho! ho!" puffed the Porpoise. "I am tickled by the grief of the Goldfish there."

"Has the Goldfish a grief?" asked King Neptune.

"He has indeed! For seven days and nights he has wept because, ho! ho! ho! because he cannot marry the Moon, surpass the Sun, and possess the world!"

"And you," said King Neptune, "have you never wept for these things?"

"Not I!" puffed the Porpoise. "What! weep for the Sun and the Moon that are nothing but two blobs in the

83

distance? Weep for the world that no one can behold? No, Father! When my dinner is in the distance, I'll weep for *that;* and when I see death coming, I'll weep for *that;* but for the rest, I say pooh!"

"Well, it takes all sorts of fish to make a sea," said King Neptune, and stooping down he picked up the Goldfish and admonished it with his finger.

"Come, child," said he, "tears may be the beginning, but they should not be the end of things. Tears will get you nowhere. Do you really wish to marry the Moon, surpass the Sun, and possess the world?"

"I do, Father, I do!" quivered the Goldfish.

"Then since there is no help for it, you must get caught in the net—do you see it floating yonder in the water? Are you afraid of it?"

"Not if it will bring me all I long for," said the Goldfish bravely.

"Risk all, and you will get your desires," promised King Neptune. He let the Goldfish dart through his fingers and saw him swim boldly to the net, which was waiting to catch what it could. As the meshes closed upon him, King Neptune stretched out his hand and slipped a second fish inside it; and then, stroking his green beard, he continued his stroll among his big and little children.

And what happened to the Goldfish?

He was drawn up into the Fisherman's boat that lay in wait above the net; and in the same cast a Silver Fish was taken, a lovely creature with a round body and silky fins like films of moonlit cloud. "There's a pretty pair!" thought the Fisherman, and he carried them home to please his little daughter. And to make her pleasure more complete, he first bought a globe of glass, and sprinkled sand and shells and tiny pebbles at the bottom, and set among them a sprig of coral and a strand of seaweed. Then he filled the globe with water, dropped in the Gold and Silver Fishes, and put the little glass world on a table in his cottage window.

The Goldfish, dazed with joy, swam towards the Silver Fish, crying, "You are the Moon come out of the sky! Oh see, how round the world is!"

And he looked through one side of the globe and saw flowers and trees in the garden. And he looked through another side of the globe and saw on the mantelpiece black and white elephants of ebony and ivory that the Fisherman had brought from foreign parts. And through another side of the globe he saw on the wall a fan of peacock's feathers, with eyes of gold and blue and green. And through the fourth side, on a bracket, he saw a little Chinese temple hung with bells. And he looked at the bottom of the globe and saw his own familiar world of coral, sand, and shells. And he looked at the top of the globe and saw a man, a woman, and a child smiling down at him over the rim.

And he gave a little jump of joy and cried to his Silver Bride:

"Oh Moonfish, I am greater than the Sun! For I give you not half, but the whole of the world, the top and the bottom and all the way round, with all the wonders that are in it and beyond it!"

And King Neptune under the sea, who had ears for all that passed, laughed in his beard and said:

"It was a shame ever to let such a tiny fellow loose in the vast ocean. He needed a world more suited to his size."

And ever since then, the world of the Goldfish has been a globe of glass.

"Little you know what this rose has cost."

Beauty and the Beast

Madame de Villeneuve

Once upon a time, in a far-off country, there lived a merchant who had been so fortunate in all his undertakings that he was enormously rich. As he had six sons and six daughters, however, who were accustomed to having everything they fancied, he did not find he had a penny too much. But misfortunes befell them. One day their house caught fire and speedily burned to the ground, with all the splendid furniture, books, pictures, gold, silver, and precious goods it contained. The father suddenly lost every ship he had upon the sea, either by dint of pirates, shipwreck, or fire. Then he heard that his clerks in distant countries, whom he had trusted entirely, had proved unfaithful. And at last from great wealth he fell into the direst poverty.

All that he had left was a little house in a desolate place at least a hundred leagues from the town, and to this he was forced to retreat. His children were in despair at the idea of leading such a different life. The daughters at first hoped their friends, who had been so numerous while they were rich, would insist on their staying in their houses, but they soon found they were left alone. Their former friends even attributed their misfortunes to their own extravagance and showed no intention of offering them any help.

So nothing was left for them but to take their departure to the cottage, which stood in the midst of a dark forest and seemed to be the most dismal place on the face of the earth. As they were too poor to have any servants, the girls had to work hard, and the sons, for their part, cultivated the fields to earn their living. Roughly clothed and living in the simplest way, the girls regretted unceasingly the luxuries and amusements of their former life. Only the youngest daughter tried to be brave and cheerful.

She had been as sad as anyone when misfortune first overtook her father, but soon recovering her natural gaiety, she set to work to make the best of things, to amuse her father and brothers as well as she could, and to persuade her sisters to join her in dancing and singing. But they would do nothing of the sort, and because she was not as doleful as themselves, they declared this miserable life was all she was fit for. But she was really far prettier and cleverer than they were. Indeed, she was so lovely she was always called Beauty.

After two years, when they were all beginning to get used to their new life, their father received news that one of his ships, which he had believed lost, had come safely into port with a rich cargo. All the sons and daughters at once thought that their poverty was at an end and wanted to set out directly for the town; but their father, who was more prudent, begged them to wait a little, and though it was harvest time, and he could ill be spared, determined to go himself to make inquiries.

Only the youngest daughter had any doubt but that they would soon again be as rich as they were before. They all loaded their father with commissions for jewels and dresses which it would have taken a fortune to buy; only Beauty, feeling sure that it was of no use, did not ask for anything. Her father, noticing her silence, said: "And what shall I bring for you, Beauty?"

"The only thing I wish for is to see you come home safely," she answered.

But this reply vexed her sisters, who fancied she was blaming them for having asked for such costly things. Her father, however, was pleased, but as he thought that at her age she certainly ought to like pretty presents, he told her to choose something.

"Well, dear Father," she said, "as you insist upon it, I beg that you will bring me a rose. I have not seen one since we came here, and I love them so much."

91

The merchant reached town as quickly as possible, only to find that his former companions, believing him to be dead, had divided his cargo between them. After six months of trouble and expense, he found himself as poor as when he started on his journey. To make matters worse, he was obliged to return in the most terrible weather. By the time he was within a few leagues of his home, he was almost exhausted with cold and fatigue. Though he knew it would take some hours to get through the forest, he resolved to go on. But night overtook him, and the deep snow and bitter frost made it impossible for his horse to carry him any farther.

Not a house was to be seen. The only shelter he could get was the hollow trunk of a great tree, and there he crouched all the night, which seemed to him the longest he had ever known. The howling of the wolves kept him awake, and when at last day broke, the falling snow had covered up every path, and he did not know which way to turn.

At length he made out some sort of path, but it was so rough and slippery that he fell down more than once. Presently it led him into an avenue of trees which ended in a splendid castle. It seemed to the merchant very strange that no snow had fallen in the avenue of orange trees, covered with flowers and fruit. When he reached the first court of the castle, he saw before him a flight of agate steps. He went up them and passed through several splendidly furnished rooms.

The pleasant warmth of the air revived him, and he felt very hungry; but there seemed to be nobody in all this vast and splendid palace. Deep silence reigned everywhere, and at last, tired of roaming through empty rooms and galleries, he stopped in a room smaller than the rest, where a clear fire was burning, and a couch was drawn up cosily before it. Thinking this must be prepared for someone who was expected, he sat down to wait till he should come and very soon fell into a sweet sleep.

When his extreme hunger wakened him after several hours, he was still alone; but a little table, with a good dinner on it, had been drawn up close to him. He lost no time in beginning his meal, hoping he might soon thank his considerate host, whoever it might be. But no one appeared, and even after another long sleep, from which he awoke completely refreshed, there was no sign of anybody, though a fresh meal of dainty cakes and fruit was prepared upon the little table at his elbow.

Because he was naturally timid, the silence began to terrify him, and he resolved to search once more through all the rooms; but it was of no use; there was no sign of life in the palace! He wondered what he should do. To amuse himself, he began pretending that all the treasures he saw were his own and considering how he would divide them among his children. Then he went down into the garden, and though it was winter everywhere else, here the sun shone, the birds sang, the flowers bloomed, and the air was soft and sweet. The merchant, in ecstasies with all he saw and heard, said to himself:

"All this must be meant for me. I will go this minute and bring my children to share all these delights."

In spite of being so cold and weary when he reached the castle, he had taken his horse to the stable and fed it. Now he thought he would saddle it for his homeward journey, and he turned down the path which led to the stable. This path had a hedge of roses on each side of it, and the merchant thought he had never seen such exquisite flowers. They reminded him of his promise to Beauty, and he stopped and had just gathered one to take to her when he was startled by a strange noise behind him. Turning round, he saw a frightful Beast, which seemed to be very angry and said in a terrible voice:

"Who told you you might gather my roses? Was it not enough that I sheltered you in my palace and was kind to you? This is the way you show your gratitude, by stealing my flowers! But your insolence shall not go unpunished."

The merchant, terrified by these furious words, dropped the fatal rose and, throwing himself on his knees, cried, "Pardon me, noble sir. I am truly grateful for your hospitality, which was so magnificent I could not imagine you would be offended by my taking such a little thing as a rose."

But the Beast's anger was not lessened by his speech. "You are very ready with excuses and flattery," he cried. "But that will not save you from the death you deserve."

Alas, thought the merchant, if my daughter Beauty could only know into what danger her rose has brought me! And in despair he began to tell the Beast all his misfortunes and the reason of his journey, not forgetting to mention Beauty's request.

"A king's ransom would hardly have procured all that my other daughters asked for," he said. "But I thought I might at least take Beauty her rose. I beg you to forgive me, for you see I meant no harm."

The Beast said, in a less furious tone, "I will forgive you on one condition—that you will give me one of your daughters."

"Ah," cried the merchant, "if I were cruel enough to buy my own life at the expense of one of my children's, what excuse could I invent to bring her here?"

"None," answered the Beast. "If she comes at all, she must come willingly. On no other condition will I have her. See if any one of them is courageous enough and loves you enough to come and save your life. You seem to be an honest man, so I will trust you to go home. I give you a month to see if any of your daughters will come back with you and stay here, to let you go free. If none of them is willing, you must come alone, after bidding them goodbye forever, for then you will belong to me. And do not imagine that you can hide from me, for if you fail to keep your word, I will come and fetch you!" added the Beast grimly.

The merchant accepted this proposal though he did not really think that any of his daughters would be persuaded to come. He promised to return at the time appointed, and then, anxious to escape from the presence of the Beast, he asked permission to set off at once. But the Beast answered that he could not go until the next day.

"Then you will find a horse ready for you," he said. "Now go and eat your supper and await my orders."

The poor merchant, more dead than alive, went back to his room, where the most delicious supper was already served on the little table drawn up before a blazing fire. But he was too terrified to eat and only tasted a few of the dishes, for fear the Beast should be angry if he did not obey his orders. When he had finished, he heard a great noise in the next room, which he knew meant that the Beast was coming. As he could do nothing to escape his visit, the only thing that remained was to seem as little afraid as possible; so when the Beast appeared and asked roughly if he had supped well, the merchant answered humbly that he had, thanks to his host's kindness. Then the Beast warned him to remember their agreement and to prepare his daughter exactly for what she had to expect.

"Do not get up tomorrow," he added, "until you see the sun and hear a golden bell ring. Then you will find your breakfast waiting for you, and the horse you are to ride will be ready in the courtyard. He will also bring you back again when you come with your daughter a month hence. Farewell. Take a rose to Beauty, and remember your promise!"

The merchant lay down until the sun rose. Then, after breakfast, he went to gather Beauty's rose and mounted his horse, which carried him off so swiftly that in an instant he had lost sight of the palace. He was still wrapped in gloomy thoughts when the horse stopped before the door of his cottage.

His sons and daughters, who had been uneasy at his long absence, rushed to meet him, eager to know the result of his journey which, seeing him mounted upon a splendid horse and wrapped in a rich mantle, they supposed to be favorable. But he hid the truth from them at first, only saying sadly to Beauty as he gave her the rose:

"Here is what you asked me to bring you. Little you know what it has cost."

But this excited their curiosity so greatly that presently he told them his adventures from beginning to end, and then they were all very unhappy. The girls lamented loudly over their lost hopes, and the sons declared their father should not return to the terrible castle, and began to make plans for killing the Beast if it should come to fetch him. But he reminded them he had promised to go back. Then the girls were very angry with Beauty and said it was all her fault. If she had asked for something sensible, this would never have happened.

Poor Beauty, much distressed, said to them, "I have indeed caused this misfortune, but who could have guessed that to ask for a rose in the middle of summer would cause so much misery? But as I did the mischief, it is only just that I should suffer for it. I will therefore go back with my father to keep his promise."

At first nobody would hear of it. Her father and brothers, who loved her dearly, declared nothing should make them let her go. But Beauty was firm. As the time drew near, she divided her little possessions between her sisters and said goodbye to everything she loved. When the fatal day came, she encouraged and cheered her father as they mounted together the horse which had brought him back. It seemed to fly rather than gallop, but so smoothly that Beauty was not frightened. Indeed, she would have enjoyed the journey, if she had not feared what might happen at the end of it. Her father still tried to persuade her to go back, but in vain.

While they were talking, the night fell. Then, to their great surprise, wonderful colored lights began to shine in all directions, and splendid fireworks blazed out before them; all the forest was illuminated. They even felt pleasantly warm, though it had been bitterly cold before. They reached the avenue of orange trees and saw that the palace was brilliantly lighted from roof to ground, and music sounded softly from the courtyard.

"The Beast must be very hungry," said Beauty, trying to laugh, "if he makes all this rejoicing over the arrival of his prey." But in spite of her anxiety, she admired all the wonderful things she saw.

When they had dismounted, her father led her to the little room he had been in before. Here they found a splendid fire burning and the table daintily spread with a delicious supper.

The merchant knew that this was meant for them, and Beauty, who was less frightened now that she had passed through so many rooms and seen nothing of the Beast, was quite willing to begin, for her long ride had made her very hungry. But they had hardly finished their meal, when the noise of the Beast's footsteps was heard approaching, and Beauty clung to her father in terror, which became all the greater when she saw how frightened he was. But when the Beast really appeared, though she trembled at the sight of him, she made a great effort to hide her horror and saluted him respectfully.

This evidently pleased the Beast. After looking at her he said, in a tone that might have struck terror into the boldest heart, though he did not seem to be angry:

"Good evening, old man. Good evening, Beauty."

The merchant was too terrified to reply, but Beauty answered sweetly, "Good evening, Beast."

"Have you come willingly?" asked the Beast. "Will you be content to stay here when your father goes away?"

Beauty answered bravely that she was quite prepared to stay.

"I am pleased with you," said the Beast. "As you have come of your own accord, you may remain. As for you, old man," he added, turning to the merchant, "at sunrise tomorrow take your departure. When the bell rings, get up quickly and eat your breakfast, and you will find the same horse waiting to take you home. But remember that you must never expect to see my palace again."

Then turning to Beauty, he said, "Take your father into the next room and help him choose gifts for your brothers and sisters. You will find two traveling trunks there; fill them as full as you can. It is only just that you should send them something very precious as a remembrance."

Then he went away, after saying, "Goodbye, Beauty; goodbye, old man." Beauty was beginning to think with great dismay of her father's departure, but she was afraid to disobey the Beast's orders. They went into the next room, which had shelves and cupboards all round it. They were greatly surprised at the riches it contained. There were splendid dresses fit for a queen, with all the ornaments to be worn with them, and when Beauty opened the cupboards, she was dazzled by the gorgeous jewels lying in heaps upon every shelf. After choosing a vast quantity, which she divided between her sisters— for she had made a heap of the wonderful dresses for each of them—she opened the last chest, which was full of gold.

"I think, Father," she said, "that, as the gold will be more useful to you, we had better take out the other things again, and fill the trunks with it."

So they did this, but the more they put in, the more room there seemed to be, and at last they put back all the jewels and dresses they had taken out, and Beauty even added as many more of the jewels as she could carry at once. Even then the trunks were not too full, but they were so heavy an elephant could not have carried them!

"The Beast was mocking us!" cried the merchant. "He pretended to give us all these things, knowing that I could not carry them away."

"Let us wait and see," answered Beauty. "I cannot believe he meant to deceive us. All we can do is to fasten them up and have them ready."

So they did this and returned to the little room where, to their astonishment, they found breakfast ready. The merchant ate his with a good appetite, as the Beast's generosity made him believe he might perhaps venture to come back soon and see Beauty. But she felt sure her father was leaving her forever, so she was very sad when the bell rang sharply for the second time and warned them that the time was come for them to part.

They went down into the courtyard, where two horses were waiting, one loaded with the two trunks, the other for him to ride. They were pawing the ground in their impatience to start, and the merchant bade Beauty a hasty farewell. As soon as he was mounted, he went off at such a pace she lost sight of him in an instant. Then Beauty began to cry and wandered sadly back to her own room. But she soon found she was very sleepy, and as she had nothing better to do, she lay down and instantly fell asleep. And then she dreamed she was walking by a brook bordered with trees and lamenting her sad fate, when a young prince, handsomer than anyone she had ever seen, and with a voice that went straight to her heart, came and said to her:

"Ah, Beauty, you are not so unfortunate as you suppose. Here you will be rewarded for all you have suffered elsewhere. Your every wish shall be gratified. Only try to find me out, no matter how I may be disguised, for I love you dearly, and in making me happy, you will find your own happiness. Be as truehearted as you are beautiful, and we shall have nothing left to wish for."

"What can I do, Prince, to make you happy?" said Beauty.

"Only be grateful," he answered, "and do not trust too much to your eyes. Above all, do not desert me until you have saved me from my cruel misery."

After this she thought she found herself in a room with a stately and beautiful lady, who said to her, "Dear Beauty, try not to regret all you have left behind you;

you are destined for a better fate. Only do not let yourself be deceived by appearances."

Beauty found her dreams so interesting that she was in no hurry to awake, but presently the clock roused her by calling her name softly twelve times. Then she rose and found her dressing table set out with everything she could possibly want, and when her toilet was finished, she found dinner waiting in the room next to hers. But dinner does not take very long when one is alone, and very soon she sat down cozily in the corner of a sofa and began to think about the charming prince she had seen in her dream.

"He said I could make him happy," said Beauty to herself. "It seems, then, that this horrible Beast keeps him a prisoner. How can I set him free? I wonder why they both told me not to trust to appearances? But after all, it was only a dream, so why should I trouble myself about it? I had better find something to do to amuse myself."

So she began to explore some of the many rooms of the palace. The first she entered was lined with mirrors. Beauty saw herself reflected on every side and thought she had never seen such a charming room. Then a bracelet which was hanging from a chandelier caught her eye, and on taking it down, she was greatly surprised to find that it held a portrait of her unknown admirer, just as she had seen him in her dream. With great delight she slipped the bracelet on her arm and went on into a gallery of pictures, where she soon found a portrait of the same handsome prince, as large as life, and so well painted that as she studied it, he seemed to smile kindly at her.

Tearing herself away from the portrait at last, she passed into a room which contained every musical instrument under the sun, and here she amused herself for a long while in trying them and singing until she was tired. The next room was a library, and she saw everything she had ever wanted to read as well as everything she had read. By this time it was growing dusk, and wax candles in diamond and ruby candlesticks lit themselves in every room.

Beauty found her supper served just at the time she preferred to have it, but she did not see anyone or hear a sound. Though her father had warned her she would be alone, she began to find it rather dull.

Presently she heard the Beast coming and wondered tremblingly if he meant to eat her now. However, he did not seem at all ferocious and only said gruffly:

"Good evening, Beauty."

She answered cheerfully and managed to conceal her terror. The Beast asked how she had been amusing herself, and she told him all the rooms she had seen. Then he asked if she thought she could be happy in his palace, and Beauty answered that everything was so beautiful she would be very hard to please if she could not be happy. After about an hour's talk, Beauty began to think the Beast was not nearly so terrible as she had supposed at first. Then he rose to leave her and said in his gruff voice:

"Do you love me, Beauty? Will you marry me?"

"Oh, what shall I say?" cried Beauty, for she was afraid to make the Beast angry by refusing.

"Say yes or no without fear," he replied.

"Oh, no, Beast," said Beauty hastily.

"Since you will not, good night, Beauty," he said.

And she answered, "Good night, Beast," very glad to find her refusal had not provoked him. After he was gone, she was very soon in bed and dreaming of her unknown prince.

She thought he came and said, "Ah, Beauty! Why are you so unkind to me? I fear I am fated to be unhappy for many a long day still."

Then her dreams changed, but the charming prince figured in them all. When morning came, her first thought was to look at the portrait and see if it was really like him, and she found it certainly was.

She decided to amuse herself in the garden, for the sun shone, and all the fountains were playing. She was astonished to find that every place was familiar to her, and presently she came to the very brook and the myrtle trees where she had first met the prince in her dream. That made her think more than ever he must be kept a prisoner by the Beast.

When she was tired, she went back to the palace and found a new room full of materials for every kind of work—ribbons to make into bows and silks to work into flowers. There was an aviary full of rare birds, which were so tame they flew to Beauty as soon as they saw her and perched upon her shoulders and her head.

"Pretty little creatures," she said, "how I wish your cage was nearer my room that I might often hear you sing!" So saying, she opened a door and found to her delight that it led into her own room, though she had thought it was on the other side of the palace.

There were more birds in a room farther on, parrots and cockatoos that could talk, and they greeted Beauty by name. Indeed, she found them so entertaining that she took one or two back to her room, and they talked to her while she was at supper. The Beast paid her his usual visit and asked the same questions as before, and then with a gruff good night he took his departure, and Beauty went to bed to dream of her mysterious prince.

The days passed swiftly in different amusements, and after a while Beauty found another strange thing in the palace, which often pleased her when she was tired of being alone. There was one room which she had not noticed particularly; it was empty, except that under each of the windows stood a very comfortable chair. The first time she had looked out of the window, it seemed a black curtain prevented her from seeing anything outside. But the second time she went into the room, happening to be tired, she sat down in one of the chairs, when instantly the curtain was rolled aside, and a most amusing pantomime was acted before her. There were dances and colored lights, music and pretty dresses, and it was all so gay that Beauty was in ecstasies. After that she tried the other seven windows in turn, and there was some new and surprising entertainment to be seen from each of them, so Beauty never could feel lonely any more. Every evening after supper, the Beast came to see her and always before saying good night asked her in his terrible voice:

"Beauty, will you marry me?"

And it seemed to Beauty, now she understood him better, that when she said, "No, Beast," he went away quite sad. Her happy dreams of the handsome young prince soon made her forget the poor Beast, and the only thing that disturbed her was being told to distrust appearances, to let her heart guide her, and not her eyes. Consider as she would, she could not understand.

So everything went on for a long time, until at last, happy as she was, Beauty began to long for the sight of her father and her brothers and sisters. One night, seeing her look very sad, the Beast asked her what was the matter. Beauty had quite ceased to be afraid of him. Now she knew he was really gentle in spite of his ferocious looks and his dreadful voice. So she answered that she wished to see her home once more. Upon hearing this, the Beast seemed sadly distressed and cried miserably:

"Ah, Beauty, have you the heart to desert an unhappy Beast like this? What more do you want to make you happy? Is it because you hate me that you want to escape?"

"No, dear Beast," answered Beauty softly, "I do not hate you, and I should be very sorry never to see you any more, but I long to see my father again. Only let me go for two months, and I promise to come back to you and stay for the rest of my life."

The Beast, who had been sighing dolefully while she spoke, now replied, "I cannot refuse you anything you ask, even though it should cost me my life. Take the four boxes you will find in the room next to your own and fill them with everything you wish to take with you. But remember your promise and come back when the two months are over, or you may have cause to repent it; for if you do not come in good time you will find your faithful Beast dead. You will not need any chariot to bring you back. Only say goodbye to all your brothers and sisters the night before you come away and, when you have gone to bed, turn this ring round upon your finger, and say firmly, 'I wish to go back to my palace and see my Beast again.' Good night, Beauty. Fear nothing, sleep peacefully, and before long you shall see your father once more."

As soon as Beauty was alone, she hastened to fill the boxes with all the rare and precious things she saw about her, and only when she was tired of heaping things into them did they seem to be full. Then she went to bed but could hardly sleep for joy. When at last she began to dream of her beloved prince, she was grieved to see him stretched upon a grassy bank, sad and weary, and hardly like himself.

"What is the matter?" she cried.

But he looked at her reproachfully and said, "How can you ask me, cruel one? Are you not leaving me to my death perhaps?"

"Ah, don't be so sorrowful!" cried Beauty. "I am only going to assure my father that I am safe and happy. I have promised the Beast faithfully I will come back, and he would die of grief if I did not keep my word!"

"What would that matter to you?" asked the prince. "Surely you would not care?"

"Indeed I should be ungrateful if I did not care for such a kind Beast," cried Beauty indignantly. "I would die to save him from pain. I assure you it is not his fault he is so ugly."

Just then a strange sound woke her—someone was speaking not very far away; and opening her eyes she found herself in a room she had never seen before, which was certainly not as splendid as those she had seen in the Beast's palace. Where could she be? She rose and dressed hastily and then saw that the boxes she had packed the night before were all in the room. Suddenly she heard her father's voice and rushed out to greet him joyfully.

Her brothers and sisters were astonished at her appearance, for they had never expected to see her again. There was no end to the questions they asked her. She had also much to hear about what had happened to them while she was away and of her father's journey home. But when they heard that she had only come to be with them for a short time and then must go back to the Beast's palace forever, they lamented loudly. Then Beauty asked her father what he thought her strange dreams meant and why the prince constantly begged her not to trust to appearances. After much consideration he answered:

"You tell me yourself that the Beast, frightful as he is, loves you dearly and deserves your love and gratitude for his gentleness and kindness. I think the prince must mean you to understand you ought to reward him by doing as he wishes, in spite of his ugliness."

Beauty could not help seeing that this seemed probable; still, when she thought of her dear prince who was so handsome, she did not feel at all inclined to marry the Beast. At any rate, for two months she need not decide but could enjoy herself with her sisters. But though they were rich now and lived in a town again and had plenty of acquaintances, Beauty found that nothing amused her very much. She often thought of the palace, where she was so happy, especially as at home she never once dreamed of her dear prince, and she felt quite sad without him.

Then her sisters seemed quite used to being without her and even found her rather in the way, so she would not have been sorry when the two months were over, but for her father and brothers, who begged her to stay and seemed so grieved at the thought of her departure that she had not the courage to say goodbye to them. Every day when she rose she meant to say it at night, and when night came she put it off again, until at last she had a dismal dream which helped her to make up her mind.

She thought she was wandering in a lonely path in the palace gardens, when she heard groans that seemed to come from some bushes hiding the entrance of a cave. Running quickly to see what could be the matter, she found the Beast stretched out upon his side, apparently dying. He reproached her faintly with being the cause of his distress, and at the same moment a stately lady appeared and said very gravely:

"Ah, Beauty, see what happens when people do not keep their promises! If you had delayed one day more, you would have found him dead."

Beauty was so terrified by this dream that the next morning she announced her intention of going back at once. That very evening she said goodbye to her father and her brothers and sisters, and as soon as she was in bed she turned her ring round upon her finger and said firmly:

"I wish to go back to my palace and see my Beast again."

Then she fell asleep instantly and only woke up to hear the clock saying, "Beauty, Beauty," twelve times in its musical voice, which told her she was really in the palace once more. Everything was just as before, and her birds were so glad to see her, but Beauty thought she had never known such a long day. She was so anxious to see the Beast again that she felt as if suppertime would never come.

But when it came, no Beast appeared. After listening and waiting for a long time, she ran down into the garden to search for him. Up and down the paths and avenues ran poor Beauty, calling him. No one answered, and not a trace of him could she find. At last, quite tired, she stopped for a minute's rest and saw that she was standing opposite the shady path she had seen in her dream. She rushed down it and, sure enough, there was the cave, and in it lay the Beast—asleep, so Beauty thought. Quite glad to have found him, she ran up and stroked his head, but to her horror he did not move or open his eyes.

"Oh, he is dead, and it is all my fault!" cried Beauty, crying bitterly.

But then, looking at him again, she fancied he still breathed. Hastily fetching some water from the nearest fountain, she sprinkled it over his face, and to her great delight he began to revive.

"Oh, Beast, how you frightened me!" she cried. "I never knew how much I loved you until just now, when I feared I was too late to save your life."

"Can you really love such an ugly creature as I am?" asked the Beast faintly. "Ah, Beauty, you came only just in time. I was dying because I thought you had forgotten your promise. But go back now and rest; I shall see you again by and by."

Beauty, who had half expected he would be angry with her, was reassured by his gentle voice and went back to the palace, where supper was awaiting her. And afterward the Beast came in as usual and talked about the time she had spent with her father, asking if she had enjoyed herself and if they had all been glad to see her.

Beauty quite enjoyed telling him all that had happened to her. When at last the time came for him to go, he asked, as he had so often asked before:

"Beauty, will you marry me?"

She answered softly, "Yes, dear Beast."

As she spoke a blaze of light sprang up before the windows of the palace; fireworks crackled and guns banged, and across the avenue of orange trees, in letters all made of fireflies, was written: *Long live the prince and his bride.*

Turning to ask the Beast what it could all mean, Beauty found he had disappeared, and in his place stood her long-loved prince! At the same moment the wheels of a chariot were heard upon the terrace, and two ladies entered the room. One of them Beauty recognized as the stately lady she had seen in her dreams; the other was so queenly that Beauty hardly knew which to greet first. But the one she already knew said to her companion:

"Well, Queen, this is Beauty, who has had the courage to rescue your son from the terrible enchantment. They love each other, and only your consent to their marriage is wanting to make them perfectly happy."

"I consent with all my heart," cried the queen. "How can I ever thank you enough, charming girl, for having restored my dear son to his natural form?" And then she tenderly embraced Beauty and the prince, who had meanwhile been greeting the fairy and receiving her congratulations.

"Now," said the fairy to Beauty, "I suppose you would like me to send for all your brothers and sisters to dance at your wedding?"

And so she did, and the marriage was celebrated the very next day with the utmost splendor, and Beauty and the prince lived happily ever after.

"My name is Prot, and this is my brother Krot."

PROT AND KROT

Polish folktale
as told by Agnes Szudek

There was once a soldier who had been away from Poland for many years fighting in the war with Sweden. When the war was over he took a ship for home and it cost him nearly all his money. By the time he arrived at the port of Danzig, he had only two coins in his pocket, a small loaf of bread in his knapsack, and nothing else.

His home was in the south near Sandomiersh, by the river Vistula, and he thought he would follow the river on foot, since he could not afford to sail or ride.

He had not gone far when he came to a churchyard where two old men sat together on a bench. They looked at the soldier as he passed by.

"Hello there, fine soldier boy!" one of them called. "God be with you."

"And with you," answered the soldier, raising his cap.

"Tell us, laddie, where you have been soldiering?" asked the second old man.

The soldier was anxious to be on his way, but he was a civil fellow, so he stopped out of politeness. "I've been in many places, fighting the Swedes," he said. "Now I'm on my way home to Sandomiersh."

"Ah, it must be good to have a home to go to," said the first old man. "Some people have all the luck in the world. My name is Prot, and this is my brother Krot."

"Yes, yes, I'm Krot and he's Prot. At least we think so, but we're never quite sure. Anyway, what does it matter? Our trouble is that we have neither home, food, nor even a penny between us."

"Well, I've only two pennies left," said the soldier, drawing the coins from his purse. "You can have them if they're any use to you." He gave the money to the old men, and their eyes twinkled with merriment as they exchanged looks.

"We won't forget you, soldier boy," they said. "It's good to know there's a little kindness left in the world."

The soldier saluted his elders and went on his way, whistling gaily. It was a long walk to Sandomiersh, and after traveling for many hours he felt tired and hungry. His old boots had trodden many battlefields and they were now so full of holes that he could hardly walk in them.

"A bite of bread's the order of the day now, I think," he said to himself, taking the rye bread from his knapsack. He was about to cut off a piece with his knife when he heard someone calling him.

"Hello there, soldier boy!"

The soldier turned his head in the direction of the river, from where the voice came, and there he saw Prot and Krot floating past on a simple raft made of bits of wood tied together with rope.

He gave them a wave, then noticed something quite extraordinary about the raft. It was moving upstream, against the current—without help from anyone! The soldier hurried alongside and called out: "Where did you find such a raft?"

"Oh, here and there. Bits and pieces we bought with the money you gave us," Prot called back.

"That's right, bits and pieces," echoed Krot. "We're still hungry. Have you got anything to eat?"

"Only a small loaf," answered the soldier. "You're welcome to share it."

"Then jump aboard. We're going your way as you see," said Prot.

"Going your way," said Krot.

So the soldier jumped on the raft, and the three of them shared the bread, which was very little indeed, and they had nothing to drink. But the old men did not complain. They were surprisingly good companions.

"Tell us, soldier boy, what would you wish for if you could have anything in the world?" asked Prot.

"Ah, that would take a lot of thought," replied the soldier, tapping his pipe to clean it out a bit. "There's not much in the world I really need."

"Surely there must be something," insisted Prot. "Treasure and a fine manor house, perhaps?"

"Oooooooh yes! Treasure and a manor house," said Krot.

"No, no, nothing like that. I wouldn't know how to be a grand gentleman. No, thank you, but I'd like a nice pipeful of tobacco and perhaps a few coins in my purse. That would satisfy me, I think," said the soldier.

"Go on, soldier boy, think harder," urged Prot. "Anything in the world."

"Yes, much harder. Anything at all," said Krot.

The soldier touched the knapsack with his foot. "Well," he said slowly, "since I don't want to own much more than a knapsack, it would be useful if it could hold anything, or even anyone, just for the asking. What do you think of that?"

"Not bad, not bad," said Prot.

"Not bad," said Krot. "Such wishes might come true."

"Oh yes," laughed the soldier. "Like pie in the sky, or wine in the brine, no doubt."

No sooner had he spoken than a big round pie appeared in the sky over their heads. Down it came and settled itself on the raft; shiny brown, crusty and filled with tender beef and vegetables. At the same time, in the water there appeared three bottles of red wine, knocking themselves against the raft as though begging to be opened.

Prot and Krot and the soldier ate the delicious pie, and washed it down with a bottle of red wine each. The soldier was astonished by the appearance of the food and drink, but he was so hungry, he ate first and thought to ask questions afterwards. As they finished their meal, the raft was nearing Sandomiersh.

"Time for you to get off," said Prot.

"Yes, off you go," said Krot.

The soldier picked up his knapsack and leapt onto the green bank. "Goodbye and thank you," he called back. "But do tell me where . . ." He looked up and down the river, but there was no raft to be seen and no Prot and Krot. The expanse of the Vistula was empty, save for a heron diving low over the water, and a kingfisher waiting motionless on a log.

"Such things could only happen in a dream," muttered the soldier, rubbing his eyes. "I must have been walking in my sleep."

He slung his small pack over his shoulder and put his pipe in his mouth, although there was no tobacco in it. As he sucked away absentmindedly, the pipe began to smoke, and the scent of sweet tobacco came from the bowl.

"Heavens above! Prot and Krot!" cried the soldier, looking about him as though he expected the two old men to be lurking in the grass. "Wherever you are, I thank you for your kindness." There was no sound in the quiet countryside, but the smoke from the pipe shaped itself into words which spelled out:

"YOUR KINDNESS IS REWARDED."

The soldier went on his way wondering who the strange old men could be. By evening he came to an inn where he thought he would ask for a drink of water, since he had no money for anything else. As he walked through the doorway, the purse in his belt began to feel heavier and heavier. On opening it he found that it was full of gold pieces! He ate a good supper of boiled beef in horseradish sauce, and cheese pancakes, and as he took a coin from his purse to pay the innkeeper, another one immediately came in its place. His second wish had come true!

Now the soldier did not know it, but sitting near him was a robber who saw the gold and made up his mind to have the purse. He waited in a dark corner outside the inn, ready to spring. When the soldier came out, night had fallen and before he knew what was happening the robber jumped out and demanded the money.

"My money?" said the surprised soldier.

"That's it! The gold in your purse. I saw it and I'll have it, or I'll have your life," snarled the robber.

The soldier thought quickly about his third wish, which might, only *might,* just come true. He decided to try it.

"I have put the purse in my knapsack," he said. "Take it by all means." Swinging his pack to the ground, he unfastened the buckle. As the robber bent down, the soldier said: "Into my knapsack and stay there."

As quick as lightning, the robber shot head first into the knapsack and was stuck fast. The soldier hoisted him onto his back and tipped him into the well in front of the inn.

"Splash!" Down he went to the bottom, and the soldier wound down the rope and the bucket. "Sit in the bucket," he shouted. "Someone may pull you up, if you're lucky," and away he went.

The night was warm and the sky was bright with a sprinkling of stars. The soldier took the road home which ran close to the castle of the king. He remembered how as a boy he used to watch hundreds of candles flickering in the windows and wonder what the royal family was doing.

Shortly before he reached the castle walls he saw a curious sight in a turnip field. There among the ripe turnips stood a round golden tent, guarded by a circle of the king's guards. On the hill above rose the royal castle without a single light shining in any of its windows. The soldier thought this strange and stopped to inquire.

"What's wrong?" he asked. "The castle looks deserted."

"So it is and likely to be for many a year," said one of the guards. "His Majesty can no longer live there."

"But why?" asked the soldier.

"Surely everyone in these parts knows by now that the castle is haunted by a demon that will not give the king peace, day or night. No one can get rid of it, no one at all, and the king can bear it no more."

"I think perhaps I may be able to help the king," said the soldier obligingly.

"I would be indebted to you all my life if you could," said the king, emerging from his tent in his nightgown.

The astonished soldier fell upon his knees. "Your Majesty, let me go to the castle tonight before I return home, and I will rid you of the demon."

"My dear fellow," said the king, straightening his nightcap, "you don't know what you are saying. You, go there alone, when I and all my courtiers could not bear it? No, no, it is too much to ask. I cannot allow it."

"Perhaps Your Majesty is fond of camping out?" ventured the soldier.

"Not in the least, dear boy! It's so unroyal, don't you see? And most uncomfortable," replied the king, patting his aching back.

"Then let me help. I only ask permission to sleep in the castle tonight, that's all."

The king could hardly refuse. He went into his tent, and returned with a huge key. "There you are," he said. "This key will open the door. Go if you must, and if you succeed, you may have any part of my kingdom you wish as a reward."

The soldier thanked the king, took the key, and went up the hill to the darkened castle. He put the key in the lock and let himself into the main hall, where he thought he would spend the night. Taking off his jacket, he put it under his head, and with his knapsack close beside him, he lay down to sleep.

He had scarcely closed his eyes when he was awakened by a shrieking and howling, and a thin high voice calling in the darkness: "Get out! Get out! This is my castle. Everybody out! Clear the way, clear the way. Not even a mouse is allowed to stay. *It is all mine!*"

The soldier opened his eyes, and by the light of the moon, he saw a small figure prancing about. It seemed to be dressed in black, with pointed ears, pointed nose, and long pointed toes. As it went about lifting its knees up to its chin, it saw the figure of the soldier in the corner.

"I said everybody out!" screamed the demon. "Out of here this instant, do you hear? *Out! Out! Out!*"

The soldier was not at all afraid. "Why should I get out?" he said, yawning. "The king has given me permission to sleep here."

"This is my castle now," replied the demon, bouncing up onto the mantelpiece and glaring down at the soldier. "If you don't go I'll—I'll turn you into a fly."

"Then I'll buzz up and down your long nose," said the soldier, lying down again as if he didn't care.

"Will you then, you impudent creature! In that case I'll turn you into a beetle," yelled the demon, stamping up and down on the mantelpiece.

The soldier simply stretched himself and said casually, "What a pleasure it will be for me then to nip all your long pointed toes."

"*What!!!* I'll turn you into a . . . a . . . a . . ."

But before the demon could think of anything else to say, the soldier stood up and said quickly, "I'll turn *you* into my knapsack this very instant and you will remain there until I let you go."

Whizz! With the speed of an arrow the demon shot off the mantelpiece, straight into the knapsack, and the soldier fastened the buckle!

"Let me out of here, whoever you are!" the demon cried.

The soldier took no notice. He put the knapsack under his jacket, put his head down on the jacket and went to sleep. He was so tired that even the violent kicking of the demon did not disturb him.

In the morning the king sent a troop of his guards to find out what had happened to the brave soldier.

The men peered through the window and saw the soldier sitting on his small pack, peacefully smoking his pipe. Still they did not dare to go in, so they tapped on the window and shouted:

"Are you all right?"

"I'm very well, thank you," replied the soldier.

"Did you see the demon?"

"Yes, of course I did," said the soldier, blowing smoke rings.

"Where is it now?" asked the soldiers, fearfully glancing about them.

"Why, I'm sitting on it," answered the soldier. "Now no more questions if you please. Go and bring me forty blacksmiths with hammers and a barrel of wine."

"Bring what?" gasped the soldiers.

"You heard me. Quickly, do as I say." The soldier was beginning to lose patience with the frightened men. Away galloped the guards and they returned two hours later with forty blacksmiths in a cart, and behind them a wagon containing forty hammers and a barrel of wine.

The soldier ordered the blacksmiths to take it in turns hammering on his knapsack, which they did without knowing why. When they were thirsty they took a drink from the barrel, then hammered away with a will.

The demon in the knapsack began to squeal with terror. "Stop it, stop it, d'you hear? You'll never hurt a demon with a hammer, or a hundred hammers, or a thousand hammers, or even a million hammers. Demons can't feel hammers—Ouch!"

"What did you say?" called the soldier above the noise.

"I said you'll never, *ouch*! Hurt me, *ouch*! Never, *oooo-heeyerooh*!!! Stop it, I can't bear it any more!" screeched the demon, who could indeed feel every single blow from the hammers.

"That's what His Majesty said about you," shouted the soldier. "If you promise to leave this land and never return, the hammering will stop. The king wishes to live at peace in his castle."

For a moment the demon said nothing, then a few extra hard blows persuaded him.

"That's enough. I promise. I promise. Have mercy on me. Let me go and I'll never come back."

The hammering stopped and the soldier opened his knapsack. "Come out," he said. A long black pointed toe emerged, then an arm, a long nose, and two green eyes looked out in fear.

"Hurry up before I change my mind," said the soldier sternly.

At once the creature sprang up like a frog and ran away at top speed, down the hill and across the fields until it disappeared in the distance.

The soldier went to the king, who was eating breakfast rolls in his tent.

"You must be the bravest soldier in my entire kingdom," he said when he heard the story.

"Not really, Your Majesty, only the most fortunate," smiled the soldier, thinking of Prot and Krot.

"Say what you like, but I shall raise you to the rank of general. Not a word! It's the very least you deserve," announced the king, offering a plate to the soldier. "Have a roll, and put one in your pocket. Now I shall keep my promise to you. Tell me which part of my kingdom you would like for your own and it shall be yours."

The soldier, who was not a greedy man, took only one roll and asked for very little. "You are most kind, sire," he said bowing. "If it pleases Your Majesty, I need only the little cottage I already own, but if my land could reach down as far as the Vistula river, a matter of three hundred yards or so, then I would be more than content."

"Ah ha! I see you are a fisherman at heart," laughed the king. "You are an easy man to please. I wish there were more like you. From this moment on, the land is yours with the Vistula as its border. And remember, you are most welcome at my castle whenever you wish to come."

The soldier thanked the king, bowed again, and went home at last to his little cottage.

Every day he went to sit on the banks of the Vistula, not, however, to fish, as the king had thought.

129

He puffed his pipe, which was always full of tobacco, and scanned the water for signs of a roughly made raft floating upstream, carrying Prot and Krot. He watched for many months and many years, but he never saw them again. He did not forget them, though, for they had given him all he needed to be happy for the rest of his life, and he lived to the age of one-hundred-and-one!

The wet park was glittering all around him.

THE HEMULEN WHO LOVED SILENCE

Tove Jansson

Once upon a time there was a hemulen who worked in a pleasure ground, which doesn't necessarily mean having a lot of fun. The hemulen's job was to punch holes in tickets, so that people wouldn't have fun more than once, and such a job is quite enough to make anyone sad if you have to do it all your life.

The hemulen punched and punched, and while punching he used to dream of the things he would do when he got his pension at last.

In case someone doesn't know what a pension is, it means that you can do what you like in all the peace you wish for, when you're old enough. At least that was how the hemulen's relatives had explained it to him.

He had terribly many relatives, a great lot of enormous, rollicking, talkative hemulens who went

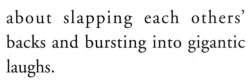

about slapping each others'
backs and bursting into gigantic
laughs.

They were joint owners of the
pleasure ground, and in their spare
time they blew the trombone or
threw the hammer, told funny
stories, and frightened people generally.
But they did it all with the best of intentions.

The hemulen himself didn't own anything because
he was on the sideline, which means only half a relative,
and as he never could put his foot down about anything
to anyone he always had to do the babysitting, to work
the big bellows of the merry-go-round, and, most of the
time, to punch tickets.

"You're lonely and have nothing to do," the other
hemulens used to tell him in their friendly way. "So it
might cheer you up a bit to lend a hand and be among
people."

"But I'm never lonely," the hemulen tried to explain.
"I can't find the time to be. There's always such a lot of
people who want to cheer me up. If you don't mind, I'd
like so much to . . ."

"Splendid," the relatives said and slapped his back.
"That's the thing. Never lonely, always on the go."

The hemulen punched along, dreaming about a great
wonderful silent loneliness, and hoped he would grow
old as soon as possible.

The whirligigs whirled, the trombones trumpeted, gaffsies and whompers and mymbles shrieked in the roller coaster every night. Edward the Booble won a first prize in china smashing, and all around the sad and dreamy hemulen people danced and whooped, laughed and quarreled, and ate and drank, and by and by the hemulen grew simply afraid of noisy people who were enjoying themselves.

He used to sleep in the hemulen children's dormitory, that was bright and nice in the daytime, and at night when the kiddies awoke and cried he comforted them with a barrel organ.

The rest of his spare time he lent a hand anywhere it was needed in a large house full of hemulens, and so he had company around the clock, and everybody was in high spirits and told him all about everything they  thought and did and planned to do. Only they never gave him time to reply properly.

"Won't I grow old soon?" the hemulen once asked at dinner.

"Old? You?" his uncle shouted. "Far from it. Buck up, buck up, nobody's older than he feels."

"But I feel really old," the hemulen said hopefully.

135

"Pish, posh," the uncle said. "We're going to have an extra spot of fireworks tonight, and the brass band will play until sunrise."

But the fireworks never were touched off, because that same afternoon a great rain started to fall. It continued all night and all the next day, and the next one after that, and then all the following week.

To tell the truth this rain kept up for eight weeks without a stop. No one had ever seen the like.

The pleasure ground lost its colors, shrunk, and withered away like a flower. It paled and rusted, and then it slowly started to disperse, because it was built on sand.

The roller coaster railway caved in with a sigh, and the merry-go-rounds went slowly turning around in large gray pools and puddles, until they were swept off, faintly tinkling, by the new rivers that were formed by the rain. All small kiddies, toffles and woodies and whompers and mymbles, and so forth, were standing days on end with their snouts pressed to the windowpanes, looking at their July becoming drenched and their color and music floating away.

The House of Mirrors came crashing
down in millions of wet splinters, and pink
drenched paper roses from the Miracle
Garden went bobbing off in hundreds
over the fields. Over it all rose the wailing
chorus of the kiddies.

They were driving their parents to
desperation, because they hadn't a single
thing to do except grieve over the lost pleasure ground.

Streamers and empty balloons were drooping from
the trees, the Happy House was filled with mud, and
the three-headed alligator swam off to the sea. He left
two of his heads behind him, because they had been
glued on.

The hemulens took it all as a splendid joke. They
stood at their windows, laughing and pointing and
slapping backs, and shouted:

"Look! There goes the curtain to the Arabian Nights!
The dancing floor has come loose! There's five black bats
from the Cave of Horror on the fillyjonk's roof! Did
you ever!"

They decided in the best of spirits to start a skating
rink instead, when the water froze, of course—and they
tried to comfort the hemulen by promising him the
ticket punching job again as soon as they could get
things going.

"No," the hemulen suddenly said. "No, no, no.
I don't want to. I want my pension. I want to do what

I feel like doing, and I want to be absolutely alone in some silent place."

"But my dear nephew," one of his uncles said with enormous astonishment, "do you mean what you say?"

"I do," said the hemulen. "Every word of it."

"But why haven't you told us before?" the perplexed relatives asked him. "We've always believed that you've enjoyed yourself."

"I never dared tell you," the hemulen admitted.

At this they all laughed again and thought it terribly funny that the hemulen had had to do things he disliked all his life, only because he hadn't been able to put his foot down.

"Well, now, what *do* you want to do?" his maternal aunt asked cheerfully.

"I'd like to build myself a doll's house," the hemulen whispered. "The most beautiful doll's house in the world, with lots and lots of rooms, and all of them silent and solemn and empty."

Now the hemulens laughed so hard that they had to sit down. They gave each other enormous nudges and shouted: "A doll's house! Did you hear that! He said a doll's house!" and then they laughed themselves into tears and told him:

"Little dear, by all means do exactly as you like! You can have grandma's big park, very probably it's silent as a grave nowadays. That's the very place for you to rummage about in and play to your heart's content. Good luck to you, and hope you like it!"

"Thanks," the hemulen said, feeling a little shrunken inwardly. "I know you've always wished me well."

His dream about the doll's house with the calm and beautiful rooms vanished; the hemulens had laughed it to pieces. But it really was no fault of theirs. They would have felt sincerely sorry if anyone had told them that they had spoiled something for the hemulen. And it's a risky thing to talk about one's most secret dreams a bit too early.

The hemulen went along to grandma's old park that was now his own. He had the key in his pocket.

The park had been closed and never used since grandma had set fire to her house with fireworks and moved elsewhere with all her family.

That was long ago, and the hemulen was even a little uncertain about the way to the park.

The wood had grown, and ways and paths were under water. While he was splashing along, the rain stopped as suddenly as it had started eight weeks ago. But the hemulen didn't notice it. He was wholly occupied with grieving over his lost dream and with feeling sorry because he didn't want to build a doll's house anymore.

Now he could see the park wall. A little of it had tumbled down, but it was still quite a high wall. The single gate was rusty and very hard to unlock.

The hemulen went in and locked the gate behind him. Suddenly he forgot about the doll's house. It was the first time in his life that he had opened a door of his own and shut it behind him. He was home. He didn't live in someone else's house.

The rain clouds were slowly drifting away and the sun came out. The wet park was steaming and glittering all around him. It was green and unworried. No one had cut or trimmed or swept it for a very, very long time. Trees were reaching branches down to the ground, bushes were climbing the trees and criss-crossing, and in the luscious grass tinkled the brooks that grandma had led through the park in her time. They didn't take care of the watering any longer, they took care only of themselves, but many of the little bridges were still standing even if the garden paths had disappeared.

The hemulen threw himself headlong into the green, friendly silence, he made capers in it, he wallowed in it, and he felt younger than he ever had before.

Oh, how wonderful to be old and pensioned at last, he thought. How much I like my relatives! And now I needn't even think of them.

He went wading through the long, sparkling grass, he threw his arms around the trees, and finally he went to sleep in the sunshine in a clearing in the middle of the park. It was the place where grandma's house had been. Her great fireworks parties were finished long ago. Young trees were coming up all around him, and in grandma's bedroom grew an enormous rosebush with a thousand red hips.

Night fell, lots of large stars came out, and the hemulen loved his park all the better. It was wide and mysterious, one could lose one's way in it and still be at home.

He wandered about for hours.

He found grandma's old fruit orchard where apples and pears lay strewn in the grass, and for a moment he thought: What a pity. I can't eat half of them. One ought to . . . And then he forgot the thought, enchanted by the loneliness of the silence.

He was the owner of the moonlight on the ground, he fell in love with the most beautiful of the trees, he made wreaths of leaves and hung them around his neck. During this first night he hardly had the heart to sleep at all.

In the morning the hemulen heard a tinkle from the old bell that still hung by the gate. He felt worried.

Someone was outside and wanted to come in, someone wanted something from him. Silently he crept in under the bushes along the wall and waited without a word. The bell jangled again. The hemulen craned his neck and saw a very small whomper waiting outside the gate.

"Go away," the hemulen called anxiously. "This is private ground. I live here."

"I know," the small whomper replied. "The hemulens sent me here with some dinner for you."

"Oh, I see, that was kind of them," the hemulen replied willingly. He unlocked the gate and took the basket from the whomper. Then he shut the gate again. The whomper remained where he was for a while but didn't say anything.

"And how are you getting on?" the hemulen asked impatiently. He stood fidgeting and longed to be back in his park again.

"Badly," the whomper replied honestly. "We're in a bad way all of us. We who are small. We've got no pleasure ground anymore. We're just grieving."

"Oh," the hemulen said, staring at his feet. He didn't want to be asked to think of dreary things, but he was so accustomed to listening that he couldn't go away either.

"You must be grieving, too," the whomper said with compassion. "You used to punch the tickets. But if one was very small and ragged and dirty you punched beside it. And we could use it two or three times."

142

"My eyesight wasn't so good," the hemulen explained. "They're waiting for you at home, aren't they?"

The whomper nodded but stayed on. He came close to the gate and thrust his snout through it. "I must tell you," he whispered. "We've got a secret."

The hemulen made a gesture of fright, because he disliked other people's secrets and confidences. But the whomper continued excitedly:

"We've rescued nearly all of it. We keep it in the fillyjonk's barn. You can't believe how much we've worked. Rescued and rescued. We stole out at nights in the rain and pulled things out of the water and down from the trees and dried them and repaired them, and now it's nearly right!"

"What is?" asked the hemulen.

"The pleasure ground of course!" the whomper cried. "Or as much of it as we could find, all the pieces there were left! Splendid, isn't it! Perhaps the hemulens will put it together again for us, and then you can come back and punch the tickets."

"Oh," the hemulen mumbled and put the basket on the ground.

"Fine, what! That made you blink," the whomper said, laughed, waved his hand, and was off.

143

Next morning the hemulen was anxiously
waiting by the gate, and when the whomper came
with the dinner basket he called at once:
"Well? What did they say?"

"They didn't want to," the whomper
said dejectedly. "They want to run a
skating rink instead. And most of us go
to sleep in winter, and anyway, where'd
we get skates from . . ."

"That's too bad," the hemulen said, feeling quite
relieved.

The whomper didn't reply, he was so disappointed.
He just put down the basket and turned back.

Poor children, the hemulen thought for a moment.
Well, well. And then he started to plan the leaf hut he
was going to build on grandma's ruins.

The hemulen worked at his building all day and
enjoyed himself tremendously. He stopped only when it
was too dark to see anything, and then he went to sleep,
tired and contented, and slept late the next morning.

When he went to the gate to fetch his food the
whomper had been there already. On the basket lid he
found a letter signed by several kiddies. "Dear pleasure
puncher," the hemulen read. "You can have all of it
because you are all right, and perhaps you will let us play
with you sometime because we like you."

The hemulen didn't understand a word, but a
horrible suspicion began burrowing in his stomach.

Then he saw. Outside the gate the kiddies had heaped all the things they had rescued from the pleasure ground. It was a lot. Most of it was broken and tattered and wrongly reassembled, and all of it looked strange. It was a lost and miscellaneous collection of boards, canvas, wire, paper, and rusty iron. It was looking sadly and unexpectantly at the hemulen, and he looked back in a panic.

Then he fled into his park and started on his leaf hut again.

He worked and worked, but nothing went quite right. His thoughts were elsewhere, and suddenly the roof came down and the hut laid itself flat on the ground.

No, said the hemulen. I don't want to. I've only just learned to say no. I'm pensioned. I do what I like. Nothing else.

He said these things several times over, more and more menacingly. Then he rose to his feet, walked through the park, unlocked the gate, and began to pull all the blessed junk and scrap inside.

The kiddies were sitting perched on the high wall around the hemulen's park. They resembled gray sparrows but were quite silent.

At times someone whispered: "What's he doing now?"

"Hush," said another. "He doesn't like to talk."

The hemulen had hung some lanterns and paper roses in the trees and turned all broken and ragged parts out of sight. Now he was assembling something that had once been a merry-go-round. The parts did not fit together very well, and half of them seemed to be missing.

"It's no use," he shouted crossly. "Can't you see? It's just a lot of scrap and nothing else! No!! I won't have any help from you."

A murmur of encouragement and sympathy was carried down from the wall, but not a word was heard.

The hemulen started to make the merry-go-round into a kind of house instead. He put the horses in the grass and the swans in the brook, turned the rest upside-down, and worked with his hair on end. Doll's house! he thought bitterly. What it all comes to in the end is a lot of tinsel and gewgaws on a dustheap, and a noise and racket like it's been all my life. . . .

Then he looked up and shouted:

"What are you staring at? Run along to the hemulens and tell them I don't want any dinner tomorrow! Instead they might send me nails and a hammer and candles and ropes and some two-inch battens, and they'd better be quick about it."

The kiddies laughed and ran off.

"Didn't we tell him," the hemulens cried and slapped each other's backs. "He has to have something to do. The poor little thing's longing for his pleasure ground."

And they sent him twice what he had asked for and, furthermore, food for a week, and ten yards of red velvet, gold and silver paper in rolls, and a barrel organ just in case.

"No," said the hemulen. "No music box. Nothing that makes a noise."

"Of course not," the kiddies said and kept the barrel organ outside.

The hemulen worked, built, and constructed. And while building he began to like the job, rather against his will. High in the trees thousands of mirror glass splinters glittered, swaying with the branches in the winds. In the treetops the hemulen made little benches and soft nests where people could sit and have a drink of juice without being observed, or just sleep. And from the strong branches hung the swings.

The roller coaster railway was difficult. It had to be only a third of its former size, because so many parts were missing. But the hemulen comforted himself with the thought that no one could be frightened enough to scream in it now. And from the last stretch one was dumped in the brook, which is great fun to most people.

But still the railway was a bit too much for the hemulen to struggle with single-handed. When he had got one side right the other side fell down, and at last he shouted, very crossly:

"Lend me a hand, someone! I can't do ten things at once all alone."

The kiddies jumped down from the wall and came running.

After this they built it jointly, and the hemulens sent them such lots of food that the kiddies were able to stay all day in the park.

In the evening they went home,
but by sunrise they stood waiting
at the gate. One morning
they had brought along the
alligator on a string.

"Are you sure he'll keep quiet?" the hemulen asked
suspiciously.

"Quite sure," the whomper replied. "He won't say a
word. He's so quiet and friendly now that he's got rid of
his other heads."

One day the fillyjonk's son found the boa constrictor
in the porcelain stove. As it behaved nicely it was
immediately brought along to grandma's park.

Everybody collected strange things for the hemulen's
pleasure ground, or simply sent him cakes, kettles,
window curtains, toffee, or whatever. It became a fad

to send along presents with the kiddies in the mornings, and the hemulen accepted everything that didn't make a noise.

But he let no one inside the wall, except the kiddies.

The park grew more and more fantastic. In the middle of it the hemulen lived in the merry-go-round house. It was gaudy and lopsided, resembling most of all a large toffee paper bag that somebody had crumpled up and thrown away.

Inside it grew the rosebush with all the red hips.

And one beautiful, mild evening all was finished. It was definitely finished, and for one moment the sadness of completion overtook the hemulen.

They had lighted the lanterns and stood looking at their work.

Mirror glass, silver, and gold gleamed in the great dark trees; everything was ready and waiting—the ponds, the boats, the tunnels, the switchback, the juice stand, the swings, the dart boards, the trees for climbing, the apple boxes . . .

"Here you are," the hemulen said. "Just remember that this is *not* a pleasure ground, it's the Park of Silence."

The kiddies silently threw themselves into the enchantment they had helped to build. But the whomper turned and asked:

"And you won't mind that you've no tickets to punch?"

"No," said the hemulen. "I'd punch the air in any case."

He went into the merry-go-round and lighted the moon from the Miracle House. Then he stretched himself out in the fillyjonk's hammock and lay looking at the stars through a hole in the ceiling.

Outside all was silent. He could hear nothing except the nearest brook and the night wind.

Suddenly the hemulen felt anxious. He sat up, listening hard. Not a sound.

Perhaps they don't have any fun at all, he thought worriedly. Perhaps they're not able to have any fun without shouting their heads off. . . . Perhaps they've gone home?

151

He took a leap up on Gaffsie's old chest of drawers and thrust his head out of a hole in the wall. No, they hadn't gone home. All the park was rustling and seething with a secret and happy life. He could hear a splash, a giggle, faint thuds and thumps, padding feet everywhere. They *were* enjoying themselves.

Tomorrow, thought the hemulen, tomorrow I'll tell them they may laugh and possibly even hum a little if they feel like it. But not more than that. Absolutely not.

He climbed down and went back to his hammock. Very soon he was asleep and not worrying over anything.

Outside the wall, by the locked gate, the hemulen's uncle was standing. He looked through the bars but saw very little.

Doesn't sound as if they had much fun, he thought. But then, everyone has to make what he can out of life. And my poor relative always was a bit queer.

He took the barrel organ home with him because he had always loved music.

"Is the story about me?" asked the Water Rat.

THE DEVOTED FRIEND

Oscar Wilde

One morning the old Water Rat put his head out of his hole. He had bright beady eyes and stiff grey whiskers, and his tail was like a long bit of black india rubber. The little ducks were swimming about in the pond, looking just like a lot of yellow canaries, and their mother, who was pure white with real red legs, was trying to teach them how to stand on their heads in the water.

"You will never be in the best society unless you can stand on your heads," she kept saying to them, and every now and then she showed them how it was done. But the little ducks paid no attention to her. They were so young that they did not know what an advantage it is to be in society at all.

"What disobedient children!" cried the old Water Rat. "They really deserve to be drowned."

"Nothing of the kind," answered the Duck. "Everyone must make a beginning, and parents cannot be too patient."

"Ah! I know nothing about the feelings of parents," said the Water Rat. "I am not a family man. In fact, I have never been married, and I never intend to be. Love is all very well in its way, but friendship is much higher. Indeed, I know of nothing in the world that is either nobler or rarer than a devoted friendship."

"And what, pray, is your idea of the duties of a devoted friend?" asked a green Linnet, who was sitting on a willow tree hard by and had overheard the conversation.

"Yes, that is just what I want to know," said the Duck, and she swam away to the end of the pond and stood upon her head, in order to give her children a good example.

"What a silly question!" cried the Water Rat. "I should expect my devoted friend to be devoted to me, of course."

"And what would you do in return?" said the little bird, swinging upon a silver spray and flapping his tiny wings.

"I don't understand you," answered the Water Rat.

"Let me tell you a story on the subject," said the Linnet.

"Is the story about me?" asked the Water Rat. "If so, I will listen to it, for I am extremely fond of fiction."

"It is applicable to you," answered the Linnet. And he flew down, and, alighting upon the bank, he told the story of The Devoted Friend.

"Once upon a time," said the Linnet, "there was an honest little fellow named Hans."

"Was he very distinguished?" asked the Water Rat.

"No," answered the Linnet, "I don't think he was distinguished at all, except for his kind heart and his funny, round, good-humoured face. He lived in a tiny cottage all by himself, and every day he worked in his garden. In all the countryside there was no garden so lovely as his. Sweet william grew there, and gillyflowers, and shepherd's purses, and fair-maids-of-France. There were damask roses, and yellow roses, lilac crocuses and gold, purple violets and white. Columbine and lady's-smock, marjoram and wild basil, the cowslip and the flower-de-luce, the daffodil and the clove pink bloomed or blossomed in their proper order as the months went by, one flower taking another flower's place, so that there were always beautiful things to look at and pleasant odours to smell.

"Little Hans had a great many friends, but the most devoted friend of all was big Hugh the Miller. Indeed, so devoted was the rich Miller to little Hans, that he would never go by his garden without leaning over the wall and plucking a large nosegay, or a handful of sweet herbs, or filling his pockets with plums and cherries if it was the fruit season.

" 'Real friends should have everything in common,' the Miller used to say, and little Hans nodded and smiled, and felt very proud of having a friend with such noble ideas.

"Sometimes, indeed, the neighbours thought it strange that the rich Miller never gave little Hans anything in return, though he had a hundred sacks of flour stored away in his mill, and six milch cows, and a large flock of woolly sheep; but Hans never troubled his head about these things, and nothing gave him greater pleasure than to listen to all the wonderful things the Miller used to say about the unselfishness of true friendship.

"So little Hans worked away in his garden. During the spring, the summer, and the autumn he was very happy, but when the winter came, and he had no fruit or flowers to bring to the market, he suffered a good deal from cold and hunger, and often had to go to bed without any supper but a few dried pears or some hard nuts. In the winter, also, he was extremely lonely, as the Miller never came to see him then.

" 'There is no good in my going to see little Hans as long as the snow lasts,' the Miller used to say to his wife, 'for when people are in trouble they should be left alone and not be bothered by visitors. That at least is my idea about friendship, and I am sure I am right. So I shall wait till the spring comes, and then I shall pay him a visit, and he will be able to give me a large basket of primroses, and that will make him so happy.'

" 'You are certainly very thoughtful about others,' answered the Wife, as she sat in her comfortable armchair by the big pinewood fire. 'Very thoughtful indeed. It is quite a treat to hear you talk about friendship. I am sure the clergyman himself could not say such beautiful things as you do, though he does live in a three-storied house and wear a gold ring on his little finger.'

" 'But could we not ask little Hans up here?' said the Miller's youngest son. 'If poor Hans is in trouble I will give him half my porridge and show him my white rabbits.'

" 'What a silly boy you are!' cried the Miller. 'I really don't know what is the use of sending you to school. You seem not to learn anything. Why, if little Hans came up here and saw our warm fire and our good supper and our great cask of red wine, he might get envious, and envy is a most terrible thing, and would spoil anybody's nature. I certainly will not allow Hans's nature to be spoiled. I am his best friend, and I will always watch over him, and see that he is not led into any temptations. Besides, if Hans came here, he might ask me to let him have some flour on credit, and that I could not do. Flour is one thing, and friendship is another, and they should not be confused. Why, the words are spelled differently, and mean quite different things. Everybody can see that.'

" 'How well you talk!' said the Miller's Wife, pouring herself out a large glass of warm ale. 'Really I feel quite drowsy. It is just like being in church.'

" 'Lots of people act well,' answered the Miller, 'but very few people talk well, which shows that talking is much the more difficult thing of the two, and much the finer thing also.' And he looked sternly across the table at his little son, who felt so ashamed of himself that he hung his head down, and grew quite scarlet and began to cry into his tea. However, he was so young that you must excuse him."

"Is that the end of the story?" asked the Water Rat.

"Certainly not," answered the Linnet, "that is the beginning."

"Then you are quite behind the age," said the Water Rat. "Every good storyteller nowadays starts with the end, and then goes on to the beginning, and concludes with the middle. That is the new method. I heard all about it the other day from a critic who was walking round the pond with a young man. He spoke of the matter at great length, and I am sure he must have been right, for he had blue spectacles and a bald head, and whenever the young man made any remark, he always answered 'Pooh!' But pray go on with your story. I like the Miller immensely. I have all kinds of beautiful sentiments myself, so there is a great sympathy between us."

"Well," said the Linnet, hopping now on one leg and now on the other, "as soon as the winter was over, and the primroses began to open their pale yellow stars, the Miller said to his Wife that he would go down and see little Hans.

" 'Why, what a good heart you have!' cried his Wife. 'You are always thinking of others. And mind you take the big basket with you for the flowers.'

"So the Miller tied the sails of the windmill together with a strong iron chain and went down the hill with the basket on his arm.

" 'Good morning, little Hans,' said the Miller.

" 'Good morning,' said Hans, leaning on his spade and smiling from ear to ear.

" 'And how have you been all the winter?' said the Miller.

" 'Well, really,' cried Hans, 'it is very good of you to ask, very good indeed. I am afraid I had rather a hard time of it, but now the spring has come, and I am quite happy, and all my flowers are doing well.'

" 'We often talked of you during the winter, Hans,' said the Miller, 'and wondered how you were getting on.'

" 'That was kind of you,' said Hans. 'I was half afraid you had forgotten me.'

" 'Hans, I am surprised at you,' said the Miller. 'Friendship never forgets. That is the wonderful thing about it. But I am afraid you won't understand the poetry of life. How lovely your primroses are looking, by-the-bye!'

" 'They are certainly very lovely,' said Hans, 'and it is a most lucky thing for me that I have so many. I am going to bring them into the market and sell them to the Burgomaster's daughter, and buy back my wheelbarrow with the money.'

" 'Buy back your wheelbarrow? You don't mean to say you have sold it? What a very stupid thing to do!'

" 'Well, the fact is,' said Hans, 'that I was obliged to. You see the winter was a very bad time for me, and I really had no money at all to buy bread with. So I first sold the silver buttons off my Sunday coat, and then I sold my silver chain, and then I sold my big pipe, and at last I sold my wheelbarrow. But I am going to buy them all back again now.'

" 'Hans,' said the Miller, 'I will give you my wheelbarrow. It is not in very good repair. Indeed, one side is gone, and there is something wrong with the wheelspokes, but in spite of that I will give it to you. I know it is very generous of me, and a great many people would think me extremely foolish for parting with it, but I am not like the rest of the world. I think that generosity is the essence of friendship, and, besides,

I have got a new wheelbarrow for myself. Yes, you may set your mind at ease, I will give you my wheelbarrow.'

" 'Well, really, that is generous of you,' said little Hans, and his funny round face glowed all over with pleasure. 'I can easily put it in repair, as I have a plank of wood in the house.'

" 'A plank of wood!' said the Miller. 'Why, that is just what I want for the roof of my barn. There is a very large hole in it, and the corn will all get damp if I don't stop it up. How lucky you mentioned it! It is quite remarkable how one good action always breeds another. I have given you my wheelbarrow, and now you are going to give me your plank. Of course, the wheelbarrow is worth far more than the plank, but true friendship never notices things like that. Pray get it at once, and I will set to work at my barn this very day.'

" 'Certainly,' cried little Hans, and he ran into the shed and dragged the plank out.

" 'It is not a very big plank,' said the Miller, looking at it, 'and I am afraid that after I have mended my barn roof there won't be any left for you to mend the wheelbarrow with; but, of course, that is not my fault. And now, as I have given you my wheelbarrow, I am sure you would like to give me some flowers in return. Here is the basket, and mind you fill it quite full.'

" 'Quite full?' said little Hans, rather sorrowfully, for it was really a very big basket, and he knew that if he filled it he would have no flowers left for the market, and he was very anxious to get his silver buttons back.

" 'Well, really,' answered the Miller, 'as I have given you my wheelbarrow, I don't think it is much to ask you for a few flowers. I may be wrong, but I should have thought that friendship, true friendship, was quite free from selfishness of any kind.'

" 'My dear friend, my best friend,' cried little Hans, 'you are welcome to all the flowers in my garden. I would much sooner have your good opinion than my silver buttons, any day.' And he ran and plucked all his pretty primroses and filled the Miller's basket.

" 'Goodbye, little Hans,' said the Miller, and he went up the hill with the plank on his shoulder and the big basket in his hand.

" 'Goodbye,' said little Hans, and he began to dig away quite merrily, he was so pleased about the wheelbarrow.

"The next day he was nailing up some honeysuckle against the porch, when he heard the Miller's voice calling to him from the road. So he jumped off the ladder, and ran down the garden, and looked over the wall.

"There was the Miller with a large sack of flour on his back.

" 'Dear little Hans,' said the Miller, 'would you mind carrying this sack of flour for me to market?'

" 'Oh, I am so sorry,' said Hans, 'but I am really very busy today. I have got all my creepers to nail up, and all my flowers to water, and all my grass to roll.'

" 'Well, really,' said the Miller, 'I think, that considering that I am going to give you my wheelbarrow, it is rather unfriendly of you to refuse.'

" 'Oh, don't say that,' cried little Hans. 'I wouldn't be unfriendly for the whole world.' And he ran in for his cap, and trudged off with the big sack on his shoulders.

"It was a very hot day, and the road was terribly dusty, and before Hans had reached the sixth milestone he was so tired that he had to sit down and rest. However, he went on bravely, and at last he reached the market. After he had waited there for some time, he sold the sack of flour for a very good price, and then he returned home at once, for he was afraid that if he stopped too late he might meet some robbers on the way.

" 'It has certainly been a hard day,' said little Hans to himself as he was going to bed, 'but I am glad I did not refuse the Miller, for he is my best friend and, besides, he is going to give me his wheelbarrow.'

"Early the next morning the Miller came down to get the money for his sack of flour, but little Hans was so tired that he was still in bed.

" 'Upon my word,' said the Miller, 'you are very lazy. Really, considering that I am going to give you my wheelbarrow, I think you might work harder. Idleness is a great sin, and I certainly don't like any of my friends to be idle or sluggish. You must not mind my speaking quite plainly to you. Of course I should not dream of doing so if I were not your friend. But what is the good of friendship if one cannot say exactly what one means? Anybody can say charming things and try to please and to flatter, but a true friend always says unpleasant things and does not mind giving pain. Indeed, if he is a really true friend he prefers it, for he knows that then he is doing good.'

" 'I am very sorry,' said little Hans, rubbing his eyes and pulling off his nightcap, 'but I was so tired that I thought I would lie in bed for a little time and listen to the birds singing. Do you know that I always work better after hearing the birds sing?'

" 'Well, I am glad of that,' said the Miller, clapping little Hans on the back, 'for I want you to come up to the mill as soon as you are dressed and mend my barn roof for me.'

"Poor little Hans was very anxious to go and work in his garden, for his flowers had not been watered for two days, but he did not like to refuse the Miller, as he was such a good friend to him.

" 'Do you think it would be unfriendly of me if I said I was busy?' he inquired in a shy and timid voice.

" 'Well, really,' answered the Miller, 'I do not think it is much to ask of you, considering that I am going to give you my wheelbarrow; but, of course, if you refuse I will go and do it myself.'

" 'Oh! on no account,' cried little Hans, and he jumped out of bed and dressed himself and went up to the barn.

"He worked there all day long, till sunset, and at sunset the Miller came to see how he was getting on.

" 'Have you mended the hole in the roof yet, little Hans?' cried the Miller in a cheery voice.

" 'It is quite mended,' answered little Hans, coming down the ladder.

" 'Ah!' said the Miller, 'there is no work so delightful as the work one does for others.'

" 'It is certainly a great privilege to hear you talk,' answered little Hans, sitting down and wiping his forehead, 'a very great privilege. But I am afraid I shall never have such beautiful ideas as you have.'

" 'Oh! they will come to you,' said the Miller, 'but you must take more pains. At present you have only the practice of friendship; someday you will have the theory also.'

" 'Do you really think I shall?' asked little Hans.

" 'I have no doubt of it,' answered the Miller, 'but now that you have mended the roof, you had better go home and rest, for I want you to drive my sheep to the mountain tomorrow.'

"Poor little Hans was afraid to say anything to this, and early the next morning the Miller brought his sheep round to the cottage, and Hans started off with them to the mountain. It took him the whole day to get there and back, and when he returned he was so tired that he went off to sleep in his chair and did not wake up till it was broad daylight.

" 'What a delightful time I shall have in my garden!' he said, and he went to work at once.

"But somehow he was never able to look after his flowers at all, for his friend the Miller was always coming round and sending him off on long errands, or getting him to help at the mill. Little Hans was very much distressed at times, as he was afraid his flowers would think he had forgotten them, but he consoled himself by the reflection that the Miller was his best friend. 'Besides,' he used to say, 'he is going to give me his wheelbarrow, and that is an act of pure generosity.'

"So little Hans worked away for the Miller, and the Miller said all kinds of beautiful things about friendship, which Hans took down in a notebook, and used to read over at night, for he was a very good scholar.

"Now it happened that one evening little Hans was sitting by his fireside when a loud rap came at the door. It was a very wild night, and the wind was blowing and roaring round the house so terribly that at first he thought it was merely the storm. But a second rap came, and then a third, louder than any of the others.

" 'It is some poor traveller,' said little Hans to himself, and he ran to the door.

"There stood the Miller with a lantern in one hand and a big stick in the other.

" 'Dear little Hans,' cried the Miller, 'I am in great trouble. My little boy has fallen off a ladder and hurt himself, and I am going for the Doctor. But he lives so far away, and it is such a bad night, that it has just occurred to me that it would be much better if you went instead of me. You know I am going to give you my wheelbarrow, and so it is only fair that you should do something for me in return.'

" 'Certainly,' cried little Hans, 'I take it quite as a compliment your coming to me, and I will start off at once. But you must lend me your lantern, as the night is so dark that I am afraid I might fall into the ditch.'

" 'I am very sorry,' answered the Miller, 'but it is my new lantern, and it would be a great loss to me if anything happened to it.'

" 'Well, never mind, I will do without it,' cried little Hans, and he took down his great fur coat, and his warm scarlet cap, and tied a muffler round his throat, and started off.

"What a dreadful storm it was! The night was so black that little Hans could hardly see, and the wind was so strong that he could hardly stand. However, he was very courageous, and after he had been walking about three hours, he arrived at the Doctor's house and knocked at the door.

" 'Who is there?' cried the Doctor, putting his head out of his bedroom window.

" 'Little Hans, Doctor.'

" 'What do you want, little Hans?'

" 'The Miller's son has fallen from a ladder and has hurt himself, and the Miller wants you to come at once.'

" 'All right!' said the Doctor. And he ordered his horse and his big boots and his lantern, and came downstairs, and rode off in the direction of the Miller's house, little Hans trudging behind him.

"But the storm grew worse and worse, and the rain fell in torrents, and little Hans could not see where he was going, or keep up with the horse. At last he lost his way and wandered off on the moor, which was a very dangerous place, as it was full of deep holes, and there poor little Hans was drowned. His body was found the next day by some goatherds, floating in a great pool of water, and was brought back by them to the cottage.

"Everybody went to little Hans's funeral, as he was so popular, and the Miller was the chief mourner.

" 'As I was his best friend,' said the Miller, 'it is only fair that I should have the best place.' So he walked at the head of the procession in a long black cloak, and every now and then he wiped his eyes with a big pocket-handkerchief.

" 'Little Hans is certainly a great loss to everyone,' said the Blacksmith when the funeral was over, and they were all seated comfortably in the inn, drinking spiced wine and eating sweet cakes.

" 'A great loss to me at any rate,' answered the Miller. 'Why, I had as good as given him my wheelbarrow, and now I really don't know what to do with it. It is very much in my way at home, and it is in such bad repair that I could not get anything for it if I sold it. I will certainly take care not to give away anything again. One certainly suffers for being generous.' "

"Well?" said the Water Rat, after a long pause.

"Well, that is the end," said the Linnet.

"But what became of the Miller?" asked the Water Rat.

"Oh! I really don't know," replied the Linnet. "And I am sure that I don't care."

"It is quite evident then that you have no sympathy in your nature," said the Water Rat.

"I am afraid that you don't quite see the moral of the story," remarked the Linnet.

"The what?" screamed the Water Rat.

"The moral."

"Do you mean to say that the story has a moral?"

"Certainly," said the Linnet.

"Well, really," said the Water Rat in a very angry manner, "I think you should have told me that before you began. If you had done so, I certainly would not have listened to you; in fact, I should have said 'Pooh,' like the critic. However, I can say it now." So he shouted out "Pooh" at the top of his voice, gave a whisk with his tail, and went back into his hole.

"And how do you like the Water Rat?" asked the Duck, who came paddling up some minutes afterwards. "He has a great many good points, but for my own part I have a mother's feelings, and I can never look at a confirmed bachelor without the tears coming into my eyes."

"I am rather afraid that I have annoyed him," answered the Linnet. "The fact is that I told him a story with a moral."

"Ah! that is always a very dangerous thing to do," said the Duck.

And I quite agree with her.

The last of the boats lagged far behind the others.

THE DANCING PRINCESSES

Walter de la Mare

There was a King of old who had twelve daughters. Some of them were fair as swans in spring, some dark as trees on a mountainside, and all were beautiful. And because the King wished to keep their beauty to himself only, they slept at night in twelve beds in one long stone chamber whose doors were closely barred and bolted.

Yet, in spite of this, as soon as the year came round to May again, and the stars and cold of winter were gone and the world was merry, at morning and every morning the soles of the twelve Princesses' slippers were found to be worn through to the very welts. It was as if they must have been dancing in them all the night long.

News of this being brought to the King, he marvelled. Unless they had wings, how could they have flown out of the palace? There was neither crevice nor cranny in the heavy doors. He spied. He set watch. It made no difference. Brand-new though the Princesses' gold and silver slippers were overnight, they were worn out at morning. He was in rage and despair.

At last this King made a decree. He decreed that anyone who, by waking and watching, by wisdom or magic, should reveal this strange secret, and where and how and when the twelve Princesses' slippers went of nights to get so worn, he should have the hand in marriage of whichever one of the Princesses he chose, and should be made the heir to the throne. As for anyone foolish enough to be so bold as to attempt such a task and fail in it, he should be whipped out of the kingdom and maybe lose his ears into the bargain. But such was the beauty of these Princesses, many a highborn stranger lost not only his heart but his ears also; and the King grew ever more moody and morose.

Now, beyond the walls of the Royal house where lived the twelve Princesses was a forest; and one summer's evening an old soldier who was travelling home from the wars met there, on his way, a beldame with a pig. This old beldame had brought her pig to the forest to feed on the beech mast and truffles, but now, try as she might, she could not prevail upon it to be caught and to return home with her to its sty.

176

She would steal up behind it with its cord in her hand, but as soon as she drew near and all but in touch of it, the pig, that meanwhile had been busily rooting in the cool loose loam, with a flick of its ears and a twinkle of its tail would scamper off out of her reach. It was almost as if its little sharp glass-green eyes could see through the pink shutters of its ears.

The old soldier watched the pig (and the red sunlight was glinting in the young green leaves of the beeches), and at last he said: "If I may make so bold, Grannie, I know a little secret about pigs. And if, as I take it, you want to catch *that* particular pig, it's yours and welcome."

The beldame, who had fingers like birds' claws and eyes black as sloes, thanked the old soldier. Fetching out a scrap of some secret root from the bottom of his knapsack, he first slowly turned his back on the pig, then stooped down and, with the bit of root between his teeth, stared earnestly at the pig from between his legs.

Presently, either by reason of the savour of the root or drawn by curiosity, the pig edged closer and closer to the old soldier until at last it actually came nosing and sidling in underneath him, as if under a bridge. Then in a trice the old soldier snatched him up by ear and tail and slipped the noose of the cord fast. The pig squealed like forty demons, but more as if in fun than in real rage.

"There we are, Grannie," said the old soldier, giving the old beldame her pig, "and here's a scrap of the root, too. There's no pig all the world over, white, black, or piebald, but after he gets one sniff of it comes for more. *That* I'll warrant you, and I'm sure you're very welcome."

The beldame, with her pig now safely at the rope's end and the scrap of root between her fingers, thanked the old soldier and asked him of his journey and whither he was going; and it was just as if, with its snout uplifted, its ears drawn forward, the nimble young pig was also listening for his answer.

The old soldier told her he was returning from the wars. "But as for where *to*, Grannie, or what for, I hardly know. For wife or children have I none, and most of my old friends must have long ago forgotten me. Not that I'm meaning to say, Grannie," says the soldier, "that *that* much matters, me being come so far and no turning back. Still, there's just *one* thing I'd like to find out before I go, and that is where the twelve young daughters of the mad old King yonder dance of nights. If I knew that, Grannie, they say I might someday sit on a throne." With that he burst out laughing, at which the pig, with a twist of its jaws (as though recalling the sweet savour of the root), flung up its three-cornered head and laughed too.

The beldame, eyeing the old soldier closely, said that what he had asked was not a hard or dangerous matter if only he would promise to do exactly what she told him. The old soldier found *that* easy enough.

"Well," said the beldame, "when you come to the palace, you'll be set to watch, and you'll be tempted to sleep. Vow a vow, then, to taste not even a crumb of the sweet cake or sip so much as a sip of the wine the Princesses will bring to you before they go to bed. Wake and watch; then follow where they lead; and here is a cloak which, come fair or foul, will make you invisible." At this the beldame took a cloak finer than spider silk from out of a small bag or pouch she wore, and gave it him.

"That hide me!" said the soldier. "Old coat, brass buttons and all?"

"Ay," said the beldame, and thanked him again for his help; and the pig coughed, and so they parted.

When she was out of sight the old soldier had another look at the magic cloak and thought over what the beldame had told him. Being by nature bold and brave, and having nothing better to do, he went off at once to the King.

The King looked at the old soldier, listened to what he said and then, with a grim smile half hidden under his beard, bade him follow him to a little stone closet hard by the long chamber where the Princesses slept. "Watch here," he said, "and if you can discover this secret, then the reward I have decreed shall be yours. If not—" He glanced up under his brows at the brave old soldier (who had no more fear in his heart than he had money in his pocket), but did not finish his sentence.

A little before nightfall, the old soldier sat himself down on a bench in the stone closet and by the light of a stub of candle began to mend his shoe.

By and by the eldest of the Princesses knocked softly on his door, smiled on him and brought him a cup of wine and a dish of sweet cakes. He thanked her. But as soon as she was gone he dribbled out the wine drip by drip into a hole between the flagstones and made crumbs of the cakes for the mice. Then he lay down and pretended to be asleep. He snored and snored, but even while he snored he was busy with his cobbler's awl boring a little hole for a peephole between the stone of the wall where he lay and the Princesses' room. At midnight all was still.

But hardly had the little owl of midnight called, *Ahoo! Ahoo! Ahoo!* when the old soldier, hearing a gentle stirring in the next room, peeped through the tiny hole he had bored in the wall. His eyes dazzled; a wondrous sight was to be seen. For the Princesses in the filmy silver of the moon were now dressing and attiring themselves in clothes that seemed not of this world but from some strange otherwhere, which they none the less took out of their own coffers and wardrobes. They seemed to be as happy as larks in the morning or like swallows chittering before they fly, laughing and whispering together while they put on these bright garments and made ready. Only one of them, the youngest, had withdrawn herself a little apart and delayed to join them, and now kept silent. Seeing this, her sisters made merry at her and asked her what ailed her.

"The others," she said, "whom our father set to watch us were young and foolish. But that old soldier has wandered all over the world and has seen many things, and it seems to me he is crafty and wise. That, sisters, is why I say, Beware!"

Still they only laughed at her. "Crafty and wise, forsooth!" said they. "Listen to his snoring! He has eaten of our sweet cakes and drunken the spiced wine, and now he will sleep sound till morning." At this the old soldier, peeping through his little bore hole in the stones, smiled to himself and went on snoring.

When they were all ready to be gone, the eldest of the Princesses clapped her hands. At this signal, and as if by magic, in the middle of the floor one wide flagstone wheeled softly upon its neighbour, disclosing an opening there, and beneath it a narrow winding flight of steps. One by one, according to age, the Princesses followed the eldest down this secret staircase, and the old soldier knew there was no time to be lost.

He flung the old beldame's cloak over his shoulders, and (as she had foretold) instantly of himself there showed not even so much as a shadow. Then, having noiselessly unbarred the door into the Princesses' bedroom, he followed the youngest of them down the stone steps.

It was dark beneath the flagstones, and the old soldier trod clumsily in his heavy shoes. And as he groped down, he stumbled and trod on the hem of the youngest Princess's dress.

"Alas, sisters, a hand is clutching at me!" she called out to her sisters.

"A hand!" mocked the eldest. "You must have caught your sleeve on a nail!"

On and down they went and out of a narrow corridor at last emerged and came full into the open air, and, following a faint track in the green turf, reached at last a wood where the trees (their bark, branches, twigs, and leaves) were all of silver and softly shimmering in a gentle light that seemed to be neither of sun nor moon nor stars. Anon they came to a second wood, and here the trees shone softly too, but these were of gold. Anon they came to a third wood, and here the trees were in fruit, and the fruits upon them were precious stones—green, blue, amber, and burning orange.

When the Princesses had all passed through this third wood, they broke out upon a hillside, and, looking down from out the leaf-fringed trees, the old soldier saw the calm waters of a lake beyond yellow sands, and drawn up on its strand twelve swan-shaped boats. And there, standing as if in wait beside them, were twelve young men that looked to be Princes. Noble and handsome young men they were.

The Princesses, having hastened down to the strand, greeted these young men one and all, and at once embarked into the twelve swan-shaped boats, the old soldier smuggling himself as gingerly as he could into the boat of the youngest. Then the Princes rowed away softly across the water toward an island that was in the midst of the lake, where was a palace, its windows shining like crystal in the wan light that bathed sky and water.

Only the last of the boats lagged far behind the others, for the old soldier sitting there invisible on the thwart, though little else but bones and sinews, weighed as heavy as a sack of stones in the boat. At last the youngest of the Princes leaned on his oars to recover his breath. "What," he sighed, "can be amiss with this boat tonight? It never rowed so heavily."

The youngest of the Princesses looked askance at him with fear in her eyes, for the boat was atilt with the weight of the old soldier and not trimmed true. Whereupon she turned her small head and looked towards that part of the boat where sat the old soldier, for there it dipped deepest in the water. In so doing, she gazed straight into his eyes, yet perceived nothing but the green water beyond. He smiled at her, and—though she knew not why—she was comforted. "Maybe," she said, turning to the Prince again and answering what he had said, "maybe you are wearied because of the heat of the evening." And he rowed on.

When they were come to the island and into the palace there, the old soldier could hardly believe his eyes, it was a scene so fair and strange and unearthly. All the long night through, to music of harp and tambour and pipe, the Princesses danced with the Princes. Danced, too, the fountains at play, with an endless singing of birds, trees and flowers blossoming, and no one seemed to weary. But as soon as the scarlet shafts of morning showed beyond these skies, they returned at once to the boats, and the Princesses were soon back safely under the King's roof again, and so fast asleep in their beds that they looked as if they had never stirred or even sighed in them the whole night long. They might be lovely images of stone.

But the old soldier slept like a hare—with one eye open. When he awoke, which was soon, he began to think over all that he had seen and heard. The longer he pondered on it, the more he was filled with astonishment. Every now and then, as if to make sure of the land of the living, he peeped with his eye through the hole in the wall, for he was almost of a mind to believe that his journey of the night before— the enchanted woods, the lake, the palace, and the music—was nothing more than the make-believe of a dream.

So, being a man of caution, he determined to say nothing at all of what had passed this first night, but to watch again a second night. When dark drew on, he once more dribbled out the spiced wine into the crannies of the stones and crumbled the sweet cakes into morsels for the mice, himself eating nothing but a crust or two of rye bread and a rind of cheese that he had in his haversack.

All happened as before. Midnight came. The Princesses rose up out of their beds, gay and brisk as fish leaping at evening out of their haunts, and soon had made ready and were gone to their trysting place at the lakeside. All was as before.

The old soldier—to make sure even surer— watched for the third night. But this night, as he followed the Princesses, first through the wood where the leaves were of silver, and next where they resembled fine gold, and last where the fruits on the boughs were all of precious stones, he broke off in each a twig. As he did so the third time, the tree faintly sighed, and the youngest Princess heard the tree sigh. Her fears of the first night, far from being lulled and at rest, had only grown sharper. She stayed a moment in the wood, looking back, and cried, "Sisters! Sisters! We are being watched. We are being followed. I heard this tree sigh, and it was in warning." But they only laughed at her.

"Sigh, forsooth!" they said. "So, too, would you, sister, if you were clad in leaves as trees are, and a little wind went through your branches."

Hearing this, in hope to reassure her, the old soldier softly wafted the three twigs he carried in the air at a little distance from the youngest's face. Sweet was the scent of them, and she smiled. That night, too, for further proof, the old soldier stole one of the gold drinking cups in the Princes' palace and hid it away with the twigs in his haversack. Then for the last time he watched the dancing and listened to the night birds' music and the noise of the fountains. But, being tired, he sat down and yawned, for he had no great wish to be young again and was happy in being himself.

Indeed, as he looked in at the Princesses, fast, fast asleep that third early morning, their dreamless faces lying waxen and placid amid the braids of their long hair upon their pillows, he even pitied them.

That very day he asked to be taken before the King and, when he was come into his presence, entreated from him a favour.

"Say on!" said the King. The old soldier then besought the King to promise that if he told the secret thing he had discovered, he would forgive the Princesses all that had gone before.

"I'd rather," he said, "be whipped three times round Your Majesty's kingdom than open my mouth else."

The King promised. Then the old soldier brought out from his haversack the three twigs of the trees—the silver and the gold and the be-gemmed—and the gold cup from the banqueting hall; and he told the King all that had befallen him.

On first hearing of this, the King fell into a rage at the thought of how his daughters had deceived him. But he remembered his promise and was pacified. He remembered, too, the decree he had made, and sent word that his daughters should be bidden into his presence. When they were come, the dark and the fair together, he frowned on them, then turned to the old soldier: "Now choose which of these deceivers you will have for wife, for such was my decree."

The old soldier, looking at them each in turn, and smiling at the youngest, waved his great hand and said: "My liege, there is this to be said: Never lived any man high or low that *deserved* a wife as gentle and fair as one of these. But in the place of enchantment I have told of, there were twelve young Princes. Well-spoken and soldierly young men they were; and if it was choosing sons I was, such are the sons I would choose. As for myself, now—if I may be so bold, and if it would be any ease to Your Majesty's mind—it being a promise, in a manner of speaking—there's one thing, me having roved the world over all my life, I'm mortal anxious to *know*—" and here he paused.

"Say on," said the King.

"Why," replied the old soldier, "what sort of thing it feels like to sit, even though but for the mite of a moment, on a throne."

On hearing this, the King grasped his beard and laughed heartily. "Easily done," he cried. "The task is to stay there."

With his own hand he led the old soldier to the throne, placed his usual crown upon his head, the Royal sceptre in his hand, and with a gesture presented him to all assembled there. There sat the old soldier, with his war-worn face, great bony hands, and lean shanks, smiling under the jewelled crown at the company. A merry scene it was.

Then the King earnestly asked the old soldier if he had anything in mind for the future, whereby he might show him his favour. Almost as if by magic, it seemed, the memory of the beldame in the forest came back into the old soldier's head, and he said: "Well, truth's truth, Your Majesty, and if there *was* such a thing in my mind, it was pigs."

"Pigs!" cried the King. "So be it, and so be it, and so be it! Pigs you shall have in plenty," said he. "And, by the walls of Jerusalem, of all the animals on God's earth there's none better—fresh, smoked, or salted."

"Ay, sir," said the old soldier, "and even better still with their plump-chapped noddles still on their shoulders and the breath of life in their bodies!"

Then the King sent for his Lord Steward and bade that seven changes of raiment should be prepared for the old soldier, and two mules saddled and bridled, and a fat purse of money put in his hand. Besides these, the King commanded that out of the countless multitude of the Royal pigs should be chosen three score of the comeliest, liveliest, and best, with two lads for their charge.

And when towards sundown a day or two after the old soldier set out from the Royal house into the forest with his laden mules, his pigs and his pig lads, besides the gifts that had been bestowed on him by the twelve noble young Princes and Princesses, he was a glad man indeed. But most he prized a worn-out gold and silver slipper which he had asked of the youngest Princess for a keepsake. This he kept in his knapsack with his magic scrap of root and other such treasures, as if for a charm.

Bou Azza watched with weird fascination.

ALLAH WILL PROVIDE

North African folktale as told by
Robert Gilstrap and Irene Estabrook

Bou Azza was an honest woodcutter who worked hard each day cutting down trees which he sold in the marketplace of a small North African village. His efforts were not highly rewarded, however, for he earned barely enough money to keep his young wife and himself in food and clothing.

Because he was getting old in body, Bou Azza wondered with each passing day how much longer he would be able to work and who would take care of him and his wife when he was too old to do so.

One afternoon as the hot sun beat down on him, Bou Azza gathered together the logs he had cut that morning, fastened them with a piece of rope, and slung them over his shoulder. Then he set out down the hill toward his tiny house on the outskirts of the village.

Before reaching his home, Bou was forced to stop and rest beneath an olive tree near the road. As he wiped the perspiration from his forehead, he suddenly noticed a horned viper curled up on the ground a few feet away from him. At first the old woodcutter was very frightened, for he knew that a bite from this reptile would surely kill him. Carefully he climbed up to a high branch of the olive tree. But after watching the snake for a few seconds, Bou Azza realized that he had nothing to fear. The snake had other interests.

On one of the lower branches of the tree, not far from where Bou Azza was sitting, there was a small bird. The snake was staring at the bird with its beady black eyes, swaying its long, slender body back and forth, and occasionally spitting out its evil-looking, forked tongue.

At first the bird did not notice the snake, but when she did, her small feathery body was seized with helpless terror. Gripping the fragile little twig on which she rested, she tried to move her wings, but they were frozen with fear. She also tried to sound an alarm, but her beak opened and shut without a sound coming out.

As the snake swayed back and forth, Bou Azza realized that the bird had been hypnotized by the viper's movements, and he watched the two animals with weird fascination.

As Bou Azza looked down, the viper held the bird in its merciless stare, swaying from side to side like the pendulum of a clock, while the helpless victim became more and more paralyzed. Then suddenly the little bird fell from the branch and landed just a few inches from the snake. As Bou Azza watched, the snake ate its prey whole—feathers and all. Then, satisfied, it crawled away looking for new victims.

Bou Azza, rested from his journey but sickened by what he had just witnessed, headed for home with his wood on his back and an idea in his head.

As Bou Azza walked home in the twilight, he thought more and more about his idea. After a time he said to himself, "I am a fool! The serpent finds much food without really working for it, thanks to Allah, whereas I, a man, must work very hard in the hottest part of the day to earn just a mouthful of food. Allah alone is good, and with his help I will be like the serpent. No longer will I work so hard to get food when the serpent gets it for nothing. So shall it be."

And continuing on his way home, Bou Azza wore an expression of contentment over the new way of life that the serpent had revealed to him.

On the following morn, instead of rising before the sun made its way into the sky, Bou Azza stayed in bed until noon. Then he took his grass mat to the rear of the house, where he sat under a fig tree.

His wife became worried at his strange behavior, and when she saw that he obviously had no plans to work for the day, she went to him and said, "Bou Azza! What is wrong with you today? Are you not going to cut wood to sell in the market?"

"No, wife," said Bou Azza as he stretched in the sun. "I will not leave my mat even if I die of hunger. Yesterday I saw a serpent finding his food without working, and I have decided that if Allah feeds the serpents, he will provide me with my bread."

His anxious wife had no idea what her husband was talking about and thought he had gone mad.

"Please get up," she cried, and she tugged at his clothing. But nothing she said or did made any difference, and when twilight came to Bou Azza's home, he was still resting on his mat.

The poor woman was sick with worry, for she had always counted on her husband for food and money. But when she realized that he would not change his mind, she hurried to the woods while there was still light to see and looked for mushrooms to sell at the market in the village.

She looked for hours, scraping away leaves, digging under fallen logs, searching everywhere. Suddenly, as she dug into some soft earth, her knife hit something hard buried beneath the surface of the ground. Rapidly she dug the dirt away and uncovered a metal cooking pot with a lid. After working for some time, she pried the lid off and discovered that the pot was filled with shimmering gold pieces.

The animals of the forest drew close to watch her struggle helplessly with the giant pot as she shouted with excitement. But it was too heavy for her to lift. She ran as fast as she could to the house, crying with happiness. "Oh, Bou Azza," she shouted. "I have found a whole pot of gold. Come with me. Help me bring it to the house."

Actually, Bou Azza was impressed with the thought of the gold. But he had made a promise to himself not to move, and now he could not lift his finger.

"Oh wife," he said, without opening his eyes. "If Allah saw fit to let you find such a treasure, surely he will give you the strength to carry it home. Personally, I have decided not to move an inch!"

This reply made his wife furious, and she ran to the house of her brothers to see if they would help her carry the pot home. Naturally her brothers were delighted with the prospect of sharing so much gold, and they ran with Bou Azza's wife to the forest and helped her carry it home.

When she and her brothers reached her house with the giant pot spilling over with gold, she felt sure that her husband would get off his mat and help her count their fortune.

"Get up, you lazy lout!" she shouted as she stood over her husband, who slept peacefully on his straw bed. "I hope you have enough energy to come and count your riches."

195

"Did I not tell you?" he said sleepily. "I am not going to lift a finger until Allah drops fortunes on my head just as he showered gifts on the serpent."

"Just as you like," the angry wife said as she filled her skirt with hundreds of heavy gold pieces and poured them over her husband's head.

"Praise be to Allah!" her husband shouted as the gold pieces fell around him. "Praise be to the one and only Allah! Do you not now see, my wife, that serpents and men are all his creatures and he does provide for all of us?"

His wife did not understand, but she did know that for the rest of their lives she and her husband would live in luxury and that Bou Azza would never have to work again.

And every time someone came to visit them, Bou Azza told them this story, ending each time with the words, "Why work? Allah will provide."

And although his listeners felt that he was wrong, no one could contradict him.

Toad came swaggering down the steps.

MR. TOAD

Kenneth Grahame

It was a bright morning in the early part of summer; the river had resumed its wonted banks and its accustomed pace, and a hot sun seemed to be pulling everything green and bushy and spiky up out of the earth towards him, as if by strings. The Mole and the Water Rat had been up since dawn very busy on matters connected with boats and the opening of the boating season; painting and varnishing, mending paddles, repairing cushions, hunting for missing boathooks, and so on; and were finishing breakfast in their little parlour and eagerly discussing their plans for the day, when a heavy knock sounded at the door.

"Bother!" said the Rat, all over egg. "See who it is, Mole, like a good chap, since you've finished."

The Mole went to attend the summons, and the Rat heard him utter a cry of surprise. Then he flung the parlour door open, and announced with much importance, "Mr. Badger!"

This was a wonderful thing, indeed, that the Badger should pay a formal call on them, or indeed on anybody. He generally had to be caught, if you wanted him badly, as he slipped quietly along a hedgerow of an early morning or a late evening, or else hunted up in his own house in the middle of the wood, which was a serious undertaking.

The Badger strode heavily into the room, and stood looking at the two animals with an expression full of seriousness. The Rat let his egg-spoon fall on the tablecloth, and sat open-mouthed.

"The hour has come!" said the Badger at last with great solemnity.

"What hour?" asked the Rat uneasily, glancing at the clock on the mantelpiece.

"*Whose* hour, you should rather say," replied the Badger. "Why, Toad's hour! The hour of Toad! I said I would take him in hand as soon as the winter was well over, and I'm going to take him in hand to-day!"

"Toad's hour, of course!" cried the Mole delightedly. "Hooray! I remember now! *We'll* teach him to be a sensible Toad!"

"This very morning," continued the Badger, taking an arm-chair, "as I learnt last night from a trustworthy source, another new and exceptionally powerful motor-car will arrive at Toad Hall on approval or return. At this very moment, perhaps, Toad is busy arraying himself in those singularly hideous habiliments so dear to him, which transform him from a (comparatively) good-looking Toad into an Object which throws any decent-minded animal that comes across it into a violent fit. We must be up and doing, ere it is too late. You two animals will accompany me instantly to Toad Hall, and the work of rescue shall be accomplished."

"Right you are!" cried the Rat, starting up. "We'll rescue the poor unhappy animal! We'll convert him! He'll be the most converted Toad that ever was before we've done with him!"

They set off up the road on their mission of mercy, Badger leading the way. Animals when in company walk in a proper and sensible manner, in single file, instead of sprawling all across the road and being of no use or support to each other in case of sudden trouble or danger.

They reached the carriage-drive of Toad Hall to find, as the Badger had anticipated, a shiny new motor-car, of great size, painted a bright red (Toad's favourite colour), standing in front of the house. As they neared the door it was flung open, and Mr. Toad, arrayed in goggles, cap, gaiters, and enormous overcoat, came swaggering down the steps, drawing on his gauntleted gloves.

"Hullo! come on, you fellows!" he cried cheerfully on catching sight of them. "You're just in time to come with me for a jolly—to come for a jolly—for a—er—jolly——"

His hearty accents faltered and fell away as he noticed the stern unbending look on the countenances of his silent friends, and his invitation remained unfinished.

The Badger strode up the steps. "Take him inside," he said sternly to his companions. Then, as Toad was hustled through the door, struggling and protesting, he turned to the chauffeur in charge of the new motor-car.

"I'm afraid you won't be wanted to-day," he said. "Mr. Toad has changed his mind. He will not require the car. Please understand that this is final. You needn't wait." Then he followed the others inside and shut the door.

"Now, then!" he said to the Toad, when the four of them stood together in the hall, "first of all, take those ridiculous things off!"

"Shan't!" replied Toad, with great spirit. "What is the meaning of this gross outrage? I demand an instant explanation."

"Take them off him, then, you two," ordered the Badger briefly.

They had to lay Toad out on the floor, kicking and calling all sorts of names, before they could get to work properly. Then the Rat sat on him, and the Mole got his motor-clothes off him bit by bit, and they stood him up on his legs again. A good deal of his blustering spirit seemed to have evaporated with the removal of his fine panoply. Now that he was merely Toad, and no longer the Terror of the Highway, he giggled feebly and looked from one to the other appealingly, seeming quite to understand the situation.

"You knew it must come to this, sooner or later, Toad," the Badger explained severely. "You've disregarded all the warnings we've given you, you've gone on squandering the money your father left you, and you're getting us animals a bad name in the district by your furious driving and your smashes and your rows with the police. Independence is all very well, but we animals never allow our friends to make fools of themselves beyond a certain limit; and that limit you've reached. Now, you're a good fellow in many respects, and I don't want to be too hard on you. I'll make one more effort to bring you to reason. You will come with me into the smoking-room, and there you will hear some facts about yourself; and we'll see whether you come out of that room the same Toad that you went in."

He took Toad firmly by the arm, led him into the smoking-room, and closed the door behind them.

"*That's* no good!" said the Rat contemptuously. "*Talking* to Toad'll never cure him. He'll *say* anything."

They made themselves comfortable in arm-chairs and waited patiently. Through the closed door they could just hear the long continuous drone of the Badger's voice, rising and falling in waves of oratory; and presently they noticed that the sermon began to be punctuated at intervals by long-drawn sobs, evidently proceeding from the bosom of Toad, who was a soft-hearted and affectionate fellow, very easily converted—for the time being—to any point of view.

After some three-quarters of an hour the door opened, and the Badger reappeared, solemnly leading by the paw a very limp and dejected Toad. His skin hung baggily about him, his legs wobbled, and his cheeks were furrowed by the tears so plentifully called forth by the Badger's moving discourse.

"Sit down there, Toad," said the Badger kindly, pointing to a chair. "My friends," he went on, "I am pleased to inform you that Toad has at last seen the error of his ways. He is truly sorry for his misguided conduct in the past, and he has undertaken to give up motor-cars entirely and forever. I have his solemn promise to that effect."

"That is very good news," said the Mole gravely. "Very good news indeed," observed the Rat dubiously, "if only—*if* only——"

He was looking very hard at Toad as he said this, and could not help thinking he perceived something vaguely resembling a twinkle in that animal's still sorrowful eye.

"There's only one thing more to be done," continued the gratified Badger. "Toad, I want you solemnly to repeat, before your friends here, what you fully admitted to me in the smoking-room just now. First, you are sorry for what you've done, and you see the folly of it all?"

There was a long, long pause. Toad looked desperately this way and that, while the other animals waited in grave silence. At last he spoke.

"No!" he said a little sullenly, but stoutly. "I'm *not* sorry. And it wasn't folly at all! It was simply glorious!"

"What?" cried the Badger, greatly scandalized. "You backsliding animal, didn't you tell me just now, in there——"

"O, yes, yes, in *there*," said Toad impatiently. "I'd have said anything in *there*. You're so eloquent, dear Badger, and so moving, and so convincing, and put all your points so frightfully well—you can do what you like with me in *there*, and you know it. But I've been searching my mind since, and going over things in it, and I find that I'm not a bit sorry or repentant really, so it's no earthly good saying I am; now, is it?"

"Then you don't promise," said the Badger, "never to touch a motor-car again?"

"Certainly not!" replied Toad emphatically. "On the contrary, I faithfully promise that the very first motor-car I see, poop-poop! off I go in it!"

"Told you so, didn't I?" observed the Rat to the Mole.

"Very well, then," said the Badger firmly, rising to his feet. "Since you won't yield to persuasion, we'll try what force can do. I feared it would come to this all along. You've often asked us three to come and stay with you, Toad, in this handsome house of yours; well, now we're going to. When we've converted you to a proper point of view we may quit, but not before. Take him upstairs, you two, and lock him up in

his bedroom, while we arrange matters between ourselves."

"It's for your own good, Toady, you know," said the Rat kindly, as Toad, kicking and struggling, was hauled up the stairs by his two faithful friends. "Think what fun we shall all have together, just as we used to, when you've quite got over this—this painful attack of yours!"

"We'll take great care of everything for you till you're well, Toad," said the Mole, "and we'll see your money isn't wasted, as it has been."

"No more of those regrettable incidents with the police, Toad," said the Rat, as they thrust him into his bedroom.

"And no more weeks in hospital, being ordered about by female nurses, Toad," added the Mole, turning the key on him.

They descended the stair, Toad shouting abuse at them through the keyhole; and the three friends then met in conference on the situation.

"It's going to be a tedious business," said the Badger, sighing. "I've never seen Toad so determined. However, we will see it out. He must never be left an instant unguarded. We shall have to take it in turns to be with him, till the poison has worked itself out of his system."

They arranged watches accordingly. Each animal took it in turns to sleep in Toad's room at night, and they divided the day up between them. At first Toad was undoubtedly very trying to his careful guardians. When his violent paroxysms possessed him he would arrange bedroom chairs in rude resemblance of a motor-car and would crouch on the foremost of them, bent forward and staring fixedly ahead, making uncouth and ghastly noises, till the climax was reached, when, turning a complete somersault, he would lie prostrate amidst the ruins of the chairs, apparently completely satisfied for the moment. As time passed, however, these painful seizures grew gradually less frequent, and his friends strove to divert his mind into fresh channels. But his interest in other matters did not seem to revive, and he grew apparently languid and depressed.

One fine morning the Rat, whose turn it was to go on duty, went upstairs to relieve Badger, whom he found fidgeting to be off and stretch his legs in a long ramble round his wood and down his earths and burrows. "Toad's still in bed," he told the Rat, outside the door. "Can't get much out of him, except, 'O, leave him alone, he wants nothing, perhaps he'll be better presently, it may pass off in time, don't be unduly anxious,' and so on. Now, you look out, Rat! When Toad's quiet and submissive, and playing at being the hero of a Sunday-school prize, then he's at his artfullest. There's sure to be something up. I know him. Well, now I must be off."

"How are you to-day, old chap?" inquired the Rat cheerfully, as he approached Toad's bedside.

He had to wait some minutes for an answer. At last a feeble voice replied, "Thank you so much, dear Ratty! So good of you to inquire! But first tell me how you are yourself, and the excellent Mole?"

"O, *we're* all right," replied the Rat. "Mole," he added incautiously, "is going out for a run round with Badger. They'll be out till luncheon-time, so you and I will spend a pleasant morning together, and I'll do my best to amuse you. Now jump up, there's a good fellow, and don't lie moping there on a fine morning like this!"

"Dear, kind Rat," murmured Toad, "how little you realise my condition, and how very far I am from 'jumping up' now—if ever! But do not trouble about me. I hate being a burden to my friends, and I do not expect to be one much longer. Indeed, I almost hope not."

"Well, I hope not, too," said the Rat heartily. "You've been a fine bother to us all this time, and I'm glad to hear it's going to stop. And in weather like this, and the boating season just beginning! It's too bad of you, Toad! It isn't the trouble we mind, but you're making us miss such an awful lot."

"I'm afraid it *is* the trouble you mind, though," replied the Toad languidly. "I can quite understand it. It's natural enough. You're tired of bothering about me.

I mustn't ask you to do anything further. I'm a nuisance, I know."

"You are, indeed," said the Rat. "But I tell you, I'd take any trouble on earth for you, if only you'd be a sensible animal."

"If I thought that, Ratty," murmured Toad, more feebly than ever, "then I would beg you—for the last time, probably—to step round to the village as quickly as possible—even now it may be too late—and fetch the doctor. But don't you bother. It's only a trouble, and perhaps we may as well let things take their course."

"Why, what do you want a doctor for?" inquired the Rat, coming closer and examining him. He certainly lay very still and flat, and his voice was weaker and his manner much changed.

"Surely you have noticed of late——" murmured Toad. "But no—why should you? Noticing things is only a trouble. To-morrow, indeed, you may be saying to yourself, 'Oh, if only I had noticed sooner! If only I had done something!' But no; it's a trouble. Never mind—forget that I asked."

"Look here, old man," said the Rat, beginning to get rather alarmed, "of course I'll fetch a doctor to you, if you really think you want him. But you can hardly be bad enough for that yet. Let's talk about something else."

"I fear, dear friend," said Toad, with a sad smile, "that 'talk' can do little in a case like this—or doctors either, for that matter; still, one must grasp at the slightest straw. And, by the way—while you are about it—I *hate* to give you additional trouble, but I happen to remember that you will pass the door—would you mind at the same time asking the lawyer to step up? It would be a convenience to me, and there are moments—perhaps I should say there is *a* moment—when one must face disagreeable tasks, at whatever cost to exhausted nature!"

"A lawyer! O, he must be really bad!" the affrighted Rat said to himself, as he hurried from the room, not forgetting, however, to lock the door carefully behind him.

Outside, he stopped to consider. The other two were far away, and he had no one to consult.

"It's best to be on the safe side," he said, on reflection. "I've known Toad fancy himself frightfully bad before, without the slightest reason; but I've never heard him ask for a lawyer! If there's nothing really the matter, the doctor will tell him he's an old ass, and cheer him up; and that will be something gained. I'd better humour him and go; it won't take very long." So he ran off to the village on his errand of mercy.

The Toad, who had hopped lightly out of bed as soon as he heard the key turned in the lock, watched him eagerly from the window till he disappeared down the carriage-drive. Then, laughing heartily, he dressed as quickly as possible in the smartest suit he could lay hands on at the moment, filled his pockets with cash which he took from a small drawer in the dressing-table, and next, knotting the sheets from his bed together and tying one end of the improvised rope around the central mullion of the handsome Tudor window which formed such a feature of his bedroom, he scrambled out, slid lightly to the ground, and, taking the opposite direction to the Rat, marched off light-heartedly, whistling a merry tune.

It was a gloomy luncheon for Rat when the Badger and the Mole at length returned, and he had to face them at table with his pitiful and unconvincing story. The Badger's caustic, not to say brutal, remarks may be imagined, and therefore passed over; but it was painful to the Rat that even the Mole, though he took his friend's side as far as possible, could not help saying, "You've been a bit of a duffer this time, Ratty! Toad, too, of all animals!"

"He did it awfully well," said the crestfallen Rat.

"He did *you* awfully well!" rejoined the Badger hotly. "However, talking won't mend matters. He's got clear away for the time, that's certain; and the worst of it is, he'll be so conceited with what he'll think is his cleverness that he may commit any folly. One comfort is, we're free now, and needn't waste any more of our precious time doing sentry-go. But we'd better continue to sleep at Toad Hall for a while longer. Toad may be brought back at any moment—on a stretcher, or between two policemen."

So spoke the Badger, not knowing what the future held in store, or how much water, and of how turbid a character, was to run under bridges before Toad should sit at ease again in his ancestral Hall.

Meanwhile, Toad, gay and irresponsible, was walking briskly along the high road, some miles from home. At first he had taken bypaths, and crossed many fields, and changed his course several time, in case of pursuit; but now, feeling by this time safe from recapture, and the sun smiling brightly on him, and all Nature joining in a chorus of approval to the song of self-praise that his own heart was singing to him, he almost danced along the road in his satisfaction and conceit.

"Smart piece of work that!" he remarked to himself, chuckling. "Brain against brute force—and brain came out on top—as it's bound to do. Poor old Ratty!

My! won't he catch it when the Badger gets back! A worthy fellow, Ratty, with many good qualities, but very little intelligence and absolutely no education. I must take him in hand someday, and see if I can make something of him."

Filled full of conceited thoughts such as these he strode along, his head in the air, till he reached a little town, where the sign of "The Red Lion," swinging across the road halfway down the main street, reminded him that he had not breakfasted that day, and that he was exceedingly hungry after his long walk. He marched into the inn, ordered the best

luncheon that could be provided at so short a notice, and sat down to eat it in the coffee-room.

He was about half-way through his meal when an only too familiar sound, approaching down the street, made him start and fall a-trembling all over. The poop-poop! drew nearer and nearer, the car could be heard to turn into the inn-yard and come to a stop, and Toad had to hold on to the leg of the table to conceal his overmastering emotion. Presently the party entered the coffee-room, hungry, talkative, and gay, voluble on their experiences of the morning and the merits of the chariot that had brought them along so well. Toad listened eagerly, all ears, for a time; at last he could stand it no longer. He slipped out of the room quietly, paid his bill at the bar, and as soon as he got outside sauntered round quietly to the inn-yard. "There cannot be any harm," he said to himself, "in my only just *looking* at it!"

The car stood in the middle of the yard, quite unattended, the stable-helps and other hangers-on being all at their dinner. Toad walked slowly round it, inspecting, criticizing, musing deeply.

"I wonder," he said to himself presently, "I wonder if this sort of car *starts* easily?"

Next moment, hardly knowing how it came about, he found he had hold of the handle and was turning it. As the familiar sound broke forth, the old passion seized on Toad and completely mastered him, body and soul. As if in a dream he found himself, somehow, seated in the driver's seat; as if in a dream, he pulled the lever and swung the car round the yard and out through the archway; and, as if in a dream, all sense of right and wrong, all fear of obvious consequences, seemed temporarily suspended. He increased his pace, and as the car devoured the street and leapt forth on the high road through the open country, he was only conscious that he was Toad once more, Toad at his best and highest, Toad the terror, the traffic-queller, the Lord of the lone trail, before whom all must give way or be smitten into nothingness and everlasting night. He chanted as he flew, and the car responded with sonorous drone; the miles were eaten up under him as he sped he knew not whither, fulfilling his instincts, living his hour, reckless of what might come to him.

To my mind," observed the Chairman of the Bench of Magistrates cheerfully, "the *only* difficulty that presents itself in this otherwise very clear case is, how we can possibly make it sufficiently hot for the incorrigible rogue and hardened ruffian whom we see cowering in the dock before us. Let me see: he has been found guilty, on the clearest evidence, first, of stealing a valuable motor-car; secondly, of driving to the public danger; and, thirdly, of gross impertinence to the rural police. Mr. Clerk, will you tell us, please, what is the very stiffest penalty we can impose for each of these offenses? Without, of course, giving the prisoner the benefit of any doubt, because there isn't any."

The clerk scratched his nose with his pen. "Some people would consider," he observed, "that stealing the motor-car was the worst offence; and so it is. But cheeking the police undoubtedly carries the severest penalty; and so it ought. Supposing you were to say twelve months for the theft, which is mild; and three years for the furious driving, which is lenient; and fifteen years for the cheek, which was pretty bad sort of cheek, judging by what we've heard from the witness-box, even if you only believe one-tenth part of what you heard, and I never believe more myself— those figures, if added together correctly, tot up to nineteen years——"

"First-rate!" said the Chairman.

"—So you had better make it a round twenty years and be on the safe side," concluded the Clerk.

"An excellent suggestion!" said the Chairman approvingly. "Prisoner! Pull yourself together and try and stand up straight. It's going to be twenty years for you this time. And mind, if you appear before us again, upon any charge whatever, we shall have to deal with you very seriously!"

Then the brutal minions of the law fell upon the hapless Toad; loaded him with chains, and dragged him from the Court House, shrieking, praying, protesting; across the market-place, where the playful populace, always as severe upon detected crime as they are sympathetic and helpful when one is merely "wanted," assailed him with jeers, carrots, and popular catch-words; past hooting school children, their innocent faces lit up with the pleasure they ever derive from the sight of a gentleman in difficulties; across the hollow-sounding drawbridge, below the spiky portcullis, under the frowning archway of the grim old castle, whose ancient towers soared high overhead; past guardrooms full of grinning soldiery off duty, past sentries who coughed in a horrid sarcastic way, because that is as much as a sentry on his post dare do to show

his contempt and abhorrence of crime; up time-worn
winding stairs, past men-at-arms in casquet
and corselet of steel, darting threatening
looks through their vizards; across
courtyards, where mastiffs strained at
their leash and pawed the air to
get at him; past ancient
warders, their halberds leant
against the wall, dozing
over a pasty and a flagon
of brown ale; on and on,
past the rack-chamber
and the thumb-screw-room,
past the turning that led
to the private scaffold,
till they reached the door of the
grimmest dungeon that lay in the heart
of the innermost keep. There at last they
paused, where an ancient jailer sat fingering a
bunch of mighty keys.

"Oddsbodikins!" said the sergeant of police, taking
off his helmet and wiping his forehead. "Rouse thee,
old loon, and take over from us this vile Toad, a
criminal of deepest guilt and matchless artfulness and
resource. Watch and ward him with all thy skill; and
mark thee well, greybeard, should aught untoward
befall, thy old head shall answer for his—and a
murrain on both of them!"

The jailer nodded grimly, laying his withered hand on the shoulder of the miserable Toad. The rusty key creaked in the lock, the great door clanged behind them; and Toad was a helpless prisoner in the remotest dungeon of the best-guarded keep of the stoutest castle in all the length and breadth of Merry England.

THE FURTHER ADVENTURES OF TOAD

Kenneth Grahame

When Toad found himself immured in a dank and noisome dungeon, and knew that all the grim darkness of a medieval fortress lay between him and the outer world of sunshine and well-metalled high roads where he had lately been so happy, disporting himself as if he had bought up every road in England, he flung himself at full length on the floor, and shed bitter tears, and abandoned himself to dark despair. "This is the end of everything" (he said), "at least it is the end of the career of Toad, which is the same thing; the popular and handsome Toad, the rich and hospitable Toad, the Toad so free and careless and debonair! How can I hope to be ever set at large again" (he said), "who have been imprisoned so justly for stealing so handsome a motor-car in such an audacious manner, and for such lurid and imaginative cheek, bestowed upon such a number of fat, red-faced policemen!" (Here his sobs choked him.) "Stupid animal that I was" (he said), "now I must languish in this dungeon, till people who were proud to say they knew me, have forgotten the very name of Toad! O wise old Badger!" (he said), "O clever, intelligent Rat and sensible Mole! What sound judgments, what a knowledge of men and matters you possess! O unhappy and forsaken Toad!" With lamentations such as these he passed his days and nights for several weeks, refusing his meals or intermediate light refreshments, though the grim and ancient jailer, knowing that Toad's pockets were well lined, frequently pointed out that many comforts, and indeed luxuries, could by arrangement be sent in—at a price—from outside.

Now the jailer had a daughter, a pleasant wench and good-hearted, who assisted her father in the lighter duties of his post. She was particularly fond of animals, and, besides her canary, whose cage hung on a nail in the massive wall of the keep by day, to the great annoyance of prisoners who relished an after-dinner nap, and was shrouded in an antimacassar on the parlour table at night, she kept several piebald mice and a restless revolving squirrel. This kind-hearted girl, pitying the misery of Toad, said to her father one day, "Father! I can't bear to see that poor beast so unhappy, and getting so thin! You let me have the managing of him. You know how fond of animals I am. I'll make him eat from my hand, and sit up, and do all sorts of things."

Her father replied that she could do what she liked with him. He was tired of Toad, and his sulks and his airs and his meanness. So that day she went on her errand of mercy, and knocked at the door of Toad's cell.

"Now, cheer up, Toad," she said coaxingly, on entering, "and sit up and dry your eyes and be a sensible animal. And do try and eat a bit of dinner. See, I've brought you some of mine, hot from the oven!"

It was bubble-and-squeak, between two plates, and its fragrance filled the narrow cell. The penetrating smell of cabbage reached the nose of Toad as he lay prostrate in his misery on the floor, and gave him the idea for a moment that perhaps life was not such a blank and desperate thing as he had imagined. But still he wailed, and kicked with his legs, and refused to be comforted. So the wise girl retired for the time, but, of course, a good deal of the smell of hot cabbage remained behind, as it will do, and Toad, between his sobs, sniffed and reflected, and gradually began to think new and inspiring thoughts: of chivalry, and poetry, and deeds still to be done; of broad meadows, and cattle browsing in them, raked by sun and wind; of kitchen-gardens, and straight herb-borders, and warm snapdragon beset by bees; and of the comforting clink of dishes set down on the table at Toad Hall, and the scrape of chair-legs on the floor as everyone pulled himself close up to his work. The air of the narrow cell took on a rosy tinge; he began to think of his friends, and how they would surely be able to do something; of lawyers, and how they would have enjoyed his case, and what an ass he had been not to get in a few; and lastly, he thought of his own great cleverness and resource, and all that he was capable of if he only gave his great mind to it; and the cure was almost complete.

When the girl returned, some hours later, she carried a tray, with a cup of fragrant tea steaming on it; and a plate piled up with very hot buttered toast, cut thick, very brown on both sides, with the butter running through the holes in it in great golden drops, like honey from the honeycomb. The smell of that buttered toast simply talked to Toad, and with no uncertain voice; talked of warm kitchens, of breakfasts on bright frosty mornings, of cosy parlour firesides on winter evenings, when one's ramble was over and slippered feet were propped on the fender;
of the purring of contented cats, and the twitter of sleepy canaries. Toad sat up on end once more, dried his eyes, sipped his tea and munched his toast, and soon began

talking freely about himself, and the house he lived in, and his doings there, and how important he was, and what a lot his friends thought of him.

The jailer's daughter saw that the topic was doing him as much good as the tea, as indeed it was, and encouraged him to go on.

"Tell me about Toad Hall," said she. "It sounds beautiful."

"Toad Hall," said the Toad proudly, "is an eligible self-contained gentleman's residence, very unique; dating in part from the fourteenth century, but replete with every modern convenience. Up-to-date sanitation. Five minutes from church, post-office, and golf-links. Suitable for——"

"Bless the animal," said the girl, laughing, "I don't want to *take* it. Tell me something *real* about it. But first wait till I fetch you some more tea and toast."

She tripped away, and presently returned with a fresh trayful; and Toad, pitching into the toast with avidity, his spirits quite restored to their usual level, told her about the boat-house, and the fish-pond, and the old walled kitchen-garden; and about the pig-styes, and the stables, and the pigeon-house, and the hen-house; and about the dairy, and the wash-house, and the china-cupboards, and the linen-presses (she liked that bit especially); and about the banqueting-hall, and the fun they had there when the other animals were gathered round the table and Toad was at his best, singing songs, telling stories, carrying on generally. Then she wanted to know about his animal-friends, and was very interested in all he had to tell her about them and how they lived, and what they did to pass their time. Of course, she did not say she was fond of animals as *pets,* because she had the sense to see that Toad would be extremely offended. When she said good night, having filled his water-jug and shaken up his straw for him, Toad was very much the same sanguine, self-satisfied animal that he had been of old. He sang a little song or two, of the sort he used to sing at his dinner-parties, curled himself up in the straw, and had an excellent night's rest and the pleasantest of dreams.

They had many interesting talks together, after that, as the dreary days went on; and the jailer's daughter grew very sorry for Toad, and thought it a great shame that a poor little animal should be locked up in prison for what seemed to her a very trivial offence. Toad, of course, in his vanity, thought that her interest in him proceeded from a growing tenderness; and he could not help half-regretting that the social gulf between them was so very wide, for she was a comely lass, and evidently admired him very much.

One morning the girl was very thoughtful, and answered at random, and did not seem to Toad to be paying proper attention to his witty sayings and sparkling comments.

"Toad," she said presently, "just listen, please. I have an aunt who is a washerwoman."

"There, there," said Toad graciously and affably, "never mind; think no more about it. *I* have several aunts who *ought* to be washerwomen."

"Do be quiet a minute, Toad," said the girl. "You talk too much, that's your chief fault, and I'm trying to think, and you hurt my head. As I said, I have an aunt who is a washerwoman; she does the washing for all the prisoners in this castle—we try to keep any paying business of that sort in the family, you understand. She takes out the washing on Monday morning, and brings it in on Friday evening. This is a Thursday. Now, this is what occurs to me: you're very rich—at least you're

227

always telling me so—and she's very poor. A few pounds wouldn't make any difference to you, and it would mean a lot to her. Now, I think if she were properly approached—squared, I believe is the word you animals use—you could come to some arrangement by which she would let you have her dress and bonnet and so on, and you could escape from the castle as the official washerwoman. You're very alike in many respects—particularly about the figure."

"We're *not*," said the Toad in a huff. "I have a very elegant figure—for what I am."

"So has my aunt," replied the girl, "for what *she* is. But have it your own way. You horrid, proud, ungrateful animal, when I'm sorry for you, and trying to help you!"

"Yes, yes, that's all right; thank you very much indeed," said the Toad hurriedly. "But look here! you wouldn't surely have Mr. Toad, of Toad Hall, going about the country disguised as a washerwoman!"

"Then you can stop here as a Toad," replied the girl with much spirit. "I suppose you want to go off in a coach-and-four!"

Honest Toad was always ready to admit himself in the wrong. "You are a good, kind, clever girl," he said, "and I am indeed a proud and a stupid toad. Introduce me to your worthy aunt, if you will be so kind, and I have no doubt that the excellent lady and I will be able to arrange terms satisfactory to both parties."

Next evening the girl ushered her aunt into Toad's cell, bearing his week's washing pinned up in a towel. The old lady had been prepared beforehand for the interview, and the sight of certain golden sovereigns that Toad had thoughtfully placed on the table in full view practically completed the matter and left little further to discuss. In return for his cash, Toad received a cotton print gown, an apron, a shawl, and a rusty black bonnet; the only stipulation the old lady made being that she should be gagged and bound and dumped down in a corner. By this not very convincing artifice, she explained, aided by picturesque fiction which she could supply herself, she hoped to retain her situation, in spite of the suspicious appearance of things.

Toad was delighted with the suggestion. It would enable him to leave the prison in some style, and with his reputation for being a desperate and dangerous fellow untarnished; and he readily helped the jailer's daughter to make her aunt appear as much as possible the victim of circumstances over which she had no control.

"Now it's your turn, Toad," said the girl. "Take off that coat and waistcoat of yours; you're fat enough as it is."

Shaking with laughter, she proceeded to "hook-and-eye" him into the cotton print gown, arranged the shawl with a professional fold, and tied the strings of the rusty bonnet under his chin.

"You're the very image of her," she giggled, "only I'm sure you never looked half so respectable in all your life before. Now, good-bye, Toad, and good luck. Go straight down the way you came up; and if anyone says anything to you, as they probably will, being but men, you can chaff back a bit, of course, but remember you're a widow woman, quite alone in the world, with a character to lose."

With a quaking heart, but as firm a footstep as he could command, Toad set forth cautiously on what seemed to be a most hare-brained and hazardous undertaking; but he was soon agreeably surprised to find how easy everything was made for him, and a little humbled at the thought that both his popularity, and the sex that seemed to inspire it, were really another's. The washerwoman's squat figure in its familiar cotton print seemed a passport for every barred door and grim gateway; even when he hesitated, uncertain as to the right turning to take, he found himself helped out of his difficulty by the warder at the next gate, anxious to be off to his tea, summoning him to come along sharp and not keep him waiting there all night. The chaff and the humorous sallies to which he was subjected, and to which, of course, he had to provide prompt and effective reply, formed, indeed, his chief danger; for Toad was an animal with a strong sense of his own dignity, and the chaff was mostly (he thought) poor and clumsy, and the humour of the sallies entirely lacking. However, he kept his temper, though with great difficulty, suited his retorts to his company and his supposed character, and did his best not to overstep the limits of good taste.

It seemed hours before he crossed the last courtyard, rejected the pressing invitations from the last guardroom, and dodged the outspread arms of the last warder, pleading with simulated passion for just one farewell embrace. But at last he heard the wicket-gate in the great outer door click behind him, felt the fresh air of the outer world upon his anxious brow, and knew that he was free!

Dizzy with the easy success of his daring exploit, he walked quickly towards the lights of the town, not knowing in the least what he should do next, only quite certain of one thing, that he must remove himself as quickly as possible from a neighbourhood where the lady he was forced to represent was so well known and so popular a character.

As he walked along, considering, his attention was caught by some red and green lights a little way off, to one side of the town, and the sound of the puffing and snorting of engines and the banging of shunted trucks fell on his ear. "Aha!" he thought, "this is a piece of luck! A railway-station is the thing I want most in the whole world at this moment; and what's more, I needn't go through the town to get it, and shan't have to support this humiliating character by repartees which, though thoroughly effective, do not assist one's sense of self-respect."

He made his way to the station accordingly, consulted a time-table, and found that a train, bound more or less in the direction of his home, was due to start in half an hour. "More luck!" said Toad, his spirits rising rapidly, and went off to the booking-office to buy his ticket.

He gave the name of the station that he knew to be nearest to the village of which Toad Hall was the principal feature, and mechanically put his fingers, in search of the necessary money, where his waistcoat pocket should have been. But here  the cotton gown, which had nobly stood by him so far, and which he had basely forgotten, intervened, and frustrated his efforts. In a sort of nightmare he struggled with the strange uncanny thing that seemed to hold his hands, turn all muscular strivings to water, and laugh at him all the time; while other travellers, forming up in a line behind, waited with impatience, making suggestions of more or less value and comments of more or less stringency and point. At last—somehow—he never rightly understood how—he burst the barriers, attained the goal, arrived at where all waistcoat pockets are eternally situated, and found— not only no money, but no pocket to hold it, and no waistcoat to hold the pocket!

To his horror he recollected that he had left both coat and waistcoat behind him in his cell, and with them his pocket-book, money, keys, watch, matches, pencil-case—all that makes life worth living, all that distinguishes the many-pocketed animal, the lord of creation, from the inferior one-pocketed or no-pocketed productions that hop or trip about permissively, unequipped for the real contest.

In his misery he made one desperate effort to carry the thing off, and, with a return to his fine old manner—a blend of the Squire and the College Don—he said, "Look here! I find I've left my purse behind. Just give me that ticket, will you, and I'll send the money on to-morrow. I'm well known in these parts."

The clerk stared at him and the rusty black bonnet a moment, and then laughed. "I should think you were pretty well known in these parts," he said, "if you've tried this game on often. Here, stand away from the window, please, madam; you're obstructing the other passengers!"

An old gentleman who had been prodding him in the back for some moments here thrust him away, and, what was worse, addressed him as his good woman, which angered Toad more than anything that had occurred that evening.

Baffled and full of despair, he wandered blindly down the platform where the train was standing, and tears trickled down each side of his nose. It was hard, he thought, to be within sight of safety and almost of home, and to be baulked by the want of a few wretched shillings and by the pettifogging mistrustfulness of paid officials. Very soon his escape would be discovered, the hunt would be up, he would be caught, reviled, loaded with chains, dragged back again to prison and bread-and-water and straw; his guards and penalties would be doubled; and O, what sarcastic remarks the girl would make! What was to be done? He was not swift of foot; his figure was unfortunately recognizable. Could he not squeeze under the seat of a carriage? He had seen this method adopted by schoolboys, when the journey-money provided by thoughtful parents had been diverted to other and better ends. As he pondered, he found himself opposite the engine, which was being oiled, wiped, and generally caressed by its affectionate driver, a burly man with an oil-can in one hand and a lump of cottonwaste in the other.

"Hullo, mother!" said the engine-driver, "what's the trouble? You don't look particularly cheerful."

"O, sir!" said Toad, crying afresh, "I am a poor unhappy washerwoman, and I've lost all my money, and can't pay for a ticket, and I *must* get home to-night somehow, and whatever I am to do I don't know. O dear, O dear!"

"That's a bad business, indeed," said the engine-driver reflectively. "Lost your money—and can't get home—and got some kids, too, waiting for you, I dare say?"

"Any amount of 'em," sobbed Toad. "And they'll be hungry—and playing with matches—and upsetting lamps, the little innocents!—and quarrelling, and going on generally. O dear, O dear!"

"Well, I'll tell you what I'll do," said the good engine-driver. "You're a washerwoman to your trade, says you. Very well, that's that. And I'm an engine-driver, as you may well see, and there's no denying it's terribly dirty work. Uses up a power of shirts, it does,

236

till my missus is fair tired of washing 'em. If you'll wash a few shirts for me when you get home, and send 'em along, I'll give you a ride on my engine. It's against the Company's regulations, but we're not so very particular in these out-of-the-way parts."

The Toad's misery turned into rapture as he eagerly scrambled up into the cab of the engine. Of course, he had never washed a shirt in his life, and couldn't if he tried and, anyhow, he wasn't going to begin; but he thought: "When I get safely home to Toad Hall, and have money again, and pockets to put it in, I will send the engine-driver enough to pay for quite a quantity of washing, and that will be the same thing, or better."

The guard waved his welcome flag, the engine-driver whistled in cheerful response, and the train moved out of the station. As the speed increased, and the Toad could see on either side of him real fields and trees, and hedges, and cows, and horses, all flying past him, and as he thought how every minute was bringing him nearer to Toad Hall, and sympathetic friends, and money to chink in his pocket, and a soft bed to sleep in, and good things to eat, and praise and admiration at the recital of his adventures and his surpassing cleverness, he began to skip up and down and shout and sing snatches of song, to the great astonishment of the engine-driver, who had come across washerwomen before, at long intervals, but never one at all like this.

They had covered many and many a mile, and Toad was already considering what he would have for supper as soon as he got home, when he noticed that the engine-driver, with a puzzled expression on his face, was leaning over the side of the engine and listening hard. Then he saw him climb onto the coals and gaze out over the top of the train; then he returned and said to Toad: "It's very strange; we're the last train running in this direction tonight, yet I could be sworn that I heard another following us!"

Toad ceased his frivolous antics at once. He became grave and depressed, and a dull pain in the lower part of his spine, communicating itself to his legs, made him want to sit down and try desperately not to think of all the possibilities.

By this time the moon was shining brightly, and the engine-driver, steadying himself on the coal, could command a view of the line behind them for a long distance.

Presently he called out, "I can see it clearly now! It is an engine, on our rails, coming along at a great pace! It looks as if we were being pursued!"

The miserable Toad, crouching in the coal-dust, tried hard to think of something to do, with dismal want of success.

"They are gaining on us fast!" cried the engine-driver. "And the engine is crowded with the queerest lot of people! Men like ancient warders, waving halberds; policemen in their helmets, waving truncheons;

and shabbily dressed men in pot-hats, obvious and unmistakable plain-clothes detectives even at this distance, waving revolvers and walking-sticks; all waving, and all shouting the same thing—'Stop, stop, stop!' "

Then Toad fell on his knees among the coals and, raising his clasped paws in supplication, cried, "Save me, only save me, dear kind Mr. Engine-driver, and I will confess everything! I am not the simple washerwoman I seem to be! I have no children waiting for me, innocent or otherwise! I am a toad—the well-known and popular Mr. Toad, a landed proprietor; I have just escaped, by my great daring and cleverness, from a loathsome dungeon into which my enemies had flung me; and if those fellows on that engine recapture me, it will be chains and bread-and-water and straw and misery once more for poor, unhappy, innocent Toad!"

The engine-driver looked down upon him very sternly, and said, "Now tell the truth; what were you put in prison for?"

"It was nothing very much," said poor Toad, colouring deeply. "I only borrowed a motor-car while the owners were at lunch; they had no need of it at the time. I didn't mean to steal it, really; but people— especially magistrates—take such harsh views of thoughtless and high-spirited actions."

The engine-driver looked very grave and said, "I fear that you have been indeed a wicked toad, and by rights

I ought to give you up to offended justice. But you are evidently in sore trouble and distress, so I will not desert you. I don't hold with motor-cars, for one thing; and I don't hold with being ordered about by policemen when I'm on my own engine, for another. And the sight of an animal in tears always makes me feel queer and softhearted. So cheer up, Toad! I'll do my best, and we may beat them yet!"

They piled on more coals, shovelling furiously; the furnace roared, the sparks flew, the engine leapt and swung, but still their pursuers slowly gained. The engine-driver, with a sigh, wiped his brow with a handful of cottonwaste, and said, "I'm afraid it's no good, Toad. You see, they are running light, and they have the better engine. There's just one thing left for us to do, and it's your only chance, so attend very carefully to what I tell you. A short way ahead of us is a long tunnel, and on the other side of that the line passes through a thick wood. Now, I will put on all the speed I can while we are running through the tunnel, but the other fellows will slow down a bit, naturally, for fear of an accident. When we are through, I will shut off steam

and put on brakes as hard as I can, and the moment it's safe to do so you must jump and hide in the wood, before they get through the tunnel and see you. Then I will go full speed ahead again, and they can chase *me* if they like, for as long as they like and as far as they like. Now mind and be ready to jump when I tell you!"

They piled on more coals, and the train shot into the tunnel, and the engine rushed and roared and rattled, till at last they shot out at the other end into fresh air and the peaceful moonlight, and saw the wood lying dark and helpful upon either side of the line. The driver shut off steam and put on brakes, the Toad got down on the step, and as the train slowed down to almost a walking pace he heard the driver call out, "Now, jump!"

Toad jumped, rolled down a short embankment, picked himself up unhurt, scrambled into the wood and hid.

Peeping out, he saw his train get up speed again and disappear at a great pace. Then out of the tunnel burst the pursuing engine, roaring and whistling, her motley crew waving their various weapons and shouting, "Stop! stop! stop!" When they were past, the Toad had a hearty laugh—for the first time since he was thrown into prison.

But he soon stopped laughing when he came to consider that it was now very late and dark and cold, and he was in an unknown wood, with no money and no chance of supper, and still far from friends and home; and the dead silence of everything, after the roar and rattle of the train, was something of a shock. He dared not leave the shelter of the trees, so he struck into the wood, with the idea of leaving the railway as far as possible behind him.

After so many weeks within walls, he found the wood strange and unfriendly and inclined, he thought, to make fun of him. Night-jars, sounding their mechanical rattle, made him think that the wood was full of searching warders, closing in on him. An owl, swooping noiselessly towards him, brushed his shoulder with its wing, making him jump with the horrid certainty that it was a hand; then flitted off, moth-like, laughing its low ho! ho! ho! which Toad thought in very poor taste. Once he met a fox, who stopped, looked him up and down in a sarcastic sort of

way, and said, "Hullo, washerwoman! Half a pair of socks and a pillow-case short this week! Mind it doesn't occur again!" and swaggered off, sniggering. Toad looked about for a stone to throw at him, but could not succeed in finding one, which vexed him more than anything. At last, cold, hungry, and tired out, he sought the shelter of a hollow tree, where with branches and dead leaves he made himself as comfortable a bed as he could, and slept soundly till the morning.

The front door of the hollow tree faced eastwards, so Toad was called at an early hour; partly by the bright sunlight streaming in on him, partly by the exceeding coldness of his toes, which made him dream that he was at home in bed in his own handsome room with the Tudor window, on a cold winter's night, and his bedclothes had got up, grumbling and protesting they couldn't stand the cold any longer, and had run downstairs to the kitchen fire to warm themselves; and he had followed, on bare feet, along miles and miles of icy stone-paved passages, arguing and beseeching them to be reasonable. He would probably have been aroused much earlier, had he not slept for some weeks on straw over stone flags, and almost forgotten the friendly feeling of thick blankets pulled well up round the chin.

Sitting up, he rubbed his eyes first and his complaining toes next, wondered for a moment where he was, looking round for familiar stone wall and little barred window; then, with a leap of the heart, remembered everything—his escape, his flight, his pursuit; remembered, first and best thing of all, that he was free!

Free! The word and the thought alone were worth fifty blankets. He was warm from end to end as he thought of the jolly world outside, waiting eagerly for him to make his triumphal entrance, ready to serve him and play up to him, anxious to help him and to keep him company, as it always had been in days of old before misfortune fell upon him. He shook himself and combed the dry leaves out of his hair with his fingers; and, his toilet complete, marched forth into the comfortable morning sun, cold but confident, hungry but hopeful, all nervous terrors of yesterday dispelled by rest and sleep and frank and heartening sunshine.

He had the world all to himself, that early summer morning. The dewy woodland, as he threaded it, was solitary and still; the green fields that succeeded the trees were his own to do as he liked with; the road itself, when he reached it, in that loneliness that was everywhere, seemed, like a stray dog, to be looking anxiously for company. Toad, however, was looking for something that could talk, and tell him clearly which way he ought to go. It is all very well, when you have a light heart, and a clear conscience, and money in your pocket, and nobody scouring the country for you to drag you off to prison again, to follow where the road beckons and points, not caring whither. The practical Toad cared very much indeed, and he could have kicked the road for its helpless silence when every minute was of importance to him.

The reserved rustic road was presently joined by a shy little brother in the shape of a canal, which took its hand and ambled along by its side in perfect confidence, but with the same tongue-tied, uncommunicative attitude towards strangers. "Bother them!" said Toad to himself. "But, anyhow, one thing's clear. They must both be coming *from* somewhere, and going *to* somewhere. You can't get over that, Toad, my boy!" So he marched on patiently by the water's edge.

Round a bend in the canal came plodding a solitary horse, stooping forward as if in anxious thought. From rope traces attached to his collar stretched a long line, taut, but dipping with his stride, the further part of it dripping pearly drops. Toad let the horse pass, and stood waiting for what the fates were sending him.

With a pleasant swirl of quiet water at its blunt bow the barge slid up alongside of him, its gaily painted gunwale level with the towing-path, its sole occupant a big stout woman wearing a linen sun-bonnet, one brawny arm laid along the tiller.

"A nice morning, ma'am!" she remarked to Toad, as she drew up level with him.

"I dare say it is, ma'am!" responded Toad politely, as he walked along the tow-path abreast of her. "I dare say it *is* a nice morning to them that's not in sore trouble, like what I am. Here's my married daughter, she sends off to me posthaste to come to her at once; so off I comes, not knowing what may be happening or going to happen, but fearing the worst, as you will understand, ma'am, if you're a mother, too. And I've left my business to look after itself—I'm in the washing and laundering line, you must know, ma'am—and I've left my young children to look after themselves, and a more mischievous and troublesome set of young imps doesn't exist, ma'am; and I've lost all my money, and lost my way, and as for what may be happening to my married daughter, why, I don't like to think of it, ma'am!"

"Where might your married daughter be living, ma'am?" asked the barge-woman.

"She lives near to the river, ma'am," replied Toad. "Close to a fine house called Toad Hall, that's somewheres hereabouts in these parts. Perhaps you may have heard of it."

"Toad Hall? Why, I'm going that way myself," replied the barge-woman. "This canal joins the river some miles further on, a little above Toad Hall;

and then it's an easy walk. You come along in the barge with me, and I'll give you a lift."

She steered the barge close to the bank, and Toad, with many humble and grateful acknowledgments, stepped lightly on board and sat down with great satisfaction. "Toad's luck again!" thought he. "I always come out on top!"

"So you're in the washing business, ma'am?" said the barge-woman politely, as they glided along. "And a very good business you've got too, I dare say, if I'm not making too free in saying so."

"Finest business in the whole county," said Toad airily. "All the gentry come to me—wouldn't go to any one else if they were paid, they know me so well. You see, I understand my work thoroughly, and attend to it all myself. Washing, ironing, clear-starching, making up gents' fine shirts for evening wear—everything's done under my own eye!"

"But surely you don't *do* all that work yourself, ma'am?" asked the barge-woman respectfully.

"O, I have girls," said Toad lightly: "twenty girls or thereabouts, always at work. But you know what *girls* are, ma'am! Nasty little hussies, that's what *I* call 'em!"

"So do I, too," said the barge-woman with great heartiness. "But I dare say you set yours to rights, the idle trollops! And are you *very* fond of washing?"

"I love it," said Toad. "I simply dote on it. Never so happy as when I've got both arms in the wash-tub.

But, then, it comes so easy to me! No trouble at all! A real pleasure, I assure you, ma'am!"

"What a bit of luck, meeting you!" observed the barge-woman thoughtfully. "A regular piece of good fortune for both of us!"

"Why, what do you mean?" asked Toad nervously.

"Well, look at me, now," replied the barge-woman. "*I* like washing, too, just the same as you do; and for that matter, whether I like it or not I have got to do all my own, naturally, moving about as I do. Now my husband, he's such a fellow for shirking his work and leaving the barge to me, that never a moment do I get for seeing to my own affairs. By rights he ought to be here now, either steering or attending to the horse, though luckily the horse has sense enough to attend to himself. Instead of which, he's gone off with the dog, to see if they can't pick up a rabbit for dinner somewhere. Says he'll catch me up at the next lock. Well, that's as may be—I don't trust him, once he gets off with that dog, who's worse than he is. But meantime, how am I to get on with my washing?"

"O, never mind about the washing," said Toad, not liking the subject. "Try and fix your mind on that rabbit. A nice fat young rabbit, I'll be bound. Got any onions?"

"I can't fix my mind on anything but my washing," said the barge-woman, "and I wonder you can be talking of rabbits, with such a joyful prospect before you. There's a heap of things of mine that you'll find in a corner of the cabin. If you'll just take one or two of the most necessary sort—I won't venture to describe them to a lady like you, but you'll recognise 'em at a glance—and put them through the wash-tub as we go along, why it'll be a pleasure to you, as you rightly say, and a real help to me. You'll find a tub handy, and soap, and a kettle on the stove, and a bucket to haul up water from the canal with. Then I shall know you're enjoying yourself, instead of sitting here idle, looking at the scenery and yawning your head off."

"Here, you let me steer!" said Toad, now thoroughly frightened, "and then you can get on with your washing your own way. I might spoil your things, or not do 'em as you like. I'm more used to gentlemen's things myself. It's my special line."

"Let you steer?" replied the barge-woman, laughing. "It takes some practice to steer a barge properly. Besides, it's dull work, and I want you to be happy. No, you shall do the washing you are so fond of, and I'll stick to the steering that I understand. Don't try and deprive me of the pleasure of giving you a treat!"

Toad was fairly cornered. He looked for escape this way and that, saw that he was too far from the bank for a flying leap, and sullenly resigned himself to his fate. "If it comes to that," he thought in desperation, "I suppose any fool can *wash*!"

He fetched tub, soap, and other necessaries from the cabin, selected a few garments at random, tried to recollect what he had seen in casual glances through laundry windows, and set to.

A long half-hour passed, and every minute of it saw Toad getting crosser and crosser. Nothing that he could do to the things seemed to please them or do them good. He tried coaxing, he tried slapping, he tried punching; they smiled back at him out of the tub unconverted, happy in their original sin. Once or twice he looked nervously over his shoulder at the barge-woman, but she appeared to be gazing out in front of her, absorbed in her steering. His back ached badly, and he noticed with dismay that his paws were beginning to get all crinkly. Now Toad was very proud of his paws. He muttered under his breath words that should never pass the lips of either washerwomen or Toads; and lost the soap, for the fiftieth time.

A burst of laughter made him straighten himself and look round. The barge-woman was leaning back and laughing unrestrainedly, till the tears ran down her cheeks.

"I've been watching you all the time," she gasped. "I thought you must be a humbug all along, from the conceited way you talked. Pretty washerwoman you are!

251

Never washed so much as a dish-clout in your life, I'll lay!"

Toad's temper, which had been simmering viciously for some time, now fairly boiled over, and he lost all control of himself.

"You common, low, *fat* barge-woman!" he shouted; "don't you dare to talk to your betters like that! Washer-woman indeed! I would have you to know that I am a Toad, a very well-known, respected, distinguished Toad! I may be under a bit of a cloud at present, but I will *not* be laughed at by a barge-woman!"

The woman moved nearer to him and peered under his bonnet keenly and closely. "Why, so you are!" she cried. "Well, I never! A horrid, nasty, crawly Toad! And in my nice clean barge, too! Now that is a thing that I will *not* have."

She relinquished the tiller for a moment. One big mottled arm shot out and caught Toad by a fore-leg, while the other gripped him fast by a hind-leg. Then the world turned suddenly upside down, the barge seemed to flit lightly across the sky, the wind whistled in his ears, and Toad found himself flying through the air, revolving rapidly as he went.

The water, when he eventually reached it with a loud splash, proved quite cold enough for his taste, though its chill was not sufficient to quell his proud spirit, or shake the heat of his furious temper. He rose to the surface spluttering, and when he had wiped the duckweed out of his eyes the first thing he saw was the fat barge-woman looking back at him over the stern of the retreating barge and laughing; and he vowed, as he coughed and choked, to be even with her.

He struck out for the shore, but the cotton gown greatly impeded his efforts, and when at length he touched land he found it hard to climb up the steep bank unassisted. He had to take a minute or two's rest to recover his breath; then gathering his wet skirts well over his arms, he started to run after the barge as fast as his legs would carry him, wild with indignation, thirsting for revenge.

The barge-woman was still laughing when he drew up level with her. "Put yourself through your mangle, washer-woman," she called out, "and iron your face and crimp it, and you'll pass for quite a decent-looking Toad!"

Toad never paused to reply. Solid revenge was what he wanted, not cheap, windy, verbal triumphs, though he had a thing or two in his mind that he would have liked to say. He saw what he wanted ahead of him. Running swiftly on he overtook the horse, unfastened the towrope and cast off, jumped lightly on the horse's back, and urged it to a gallop by kicking it vigorously in the sides. He steered for the open country, abandoning the towpath, and swinging his steed down a rutty lane. Once he looked back, and saw that the

barge had run aground on the other side of the canal, and the barge-woman was gesticulating wildly and shouting, "Stop, stop, stop!" "I've heard that song before," said Toad, laughing, as he continued to spur his steed onward in its wild career.

The barge-horse was not capable of any very sustained effort, and its gallop soon subsided into a trot, and its trot into an easy walk; but Toad was quite contented with this, knowing that he, at any rate, was moving, and the barge was not. He had quite recovered his temper, now that he had done something he thought really clever; and he was satisfied to jog along quietly in the sun, taking advantage of any byways and bridle-paths, and trying to forget how very long it was since he had had a square meal, till the canal had been left very far behind him.

He had travelled some miles, his horse and he, and he was feeling drowsy in the hot sunshine, when the horse stopped, lowered his head, and began to nibble the grass; and Toad, waking up, just saved himself from falling off by an effort. He looked about him and found he was on a wide common, dotted with patches of gorse and bramble as far as he could see.

Near him stood a dingy gipsy caravan, and beside it a man was sitting on a bucket turned upside down, very busy smoking and staring into the wide world. A fire of sticks was burning nearby, and over the fire hung an iron pot, and out of that pot came forth bubblings and gurglings, and a vague suggestive steaminess. Also smells—warm, rich, and varied smells—that twined and twisted and wreathed themselves at last into one complete, voluptuous, perfect smell that seemed like the very soul of Nature taking form and appearing to her children, a true Goddess, a mother of solace and comfort. Toad now knew well that he had not been really hungry before. What he had felt earlier in the day had been a mere trifling qualm. This was the real thing at last, and no mistake; and it would have to be dealt with speedily, too, or there would be trouble for somebody or something. He looked the gipsy over carefully, wondering vaguely whether it would be easier to fight him or cajole him. So there he sat, and sniffed and sniffed, and looked at the gipsy; and the gipsy sat and smoked, and looked at him.

Presently the gipsy took his pipe out of his mouth and remarked in a careless way, "Want to sell that there horse of yours?"

Toad was completely taken aback. He did not know that gipsies were very fond of horse-dealing, and never missed an opportunity, and he had not reflected that caravans were always on the move and took a deal of drawing. It had not occurred to him to turn the horse into cash, but the gipsy's suggestion seemed to smooth the way towards the two things he wanted so badly— ready money and a solid breakfast.

"What?" he said, "me sell this beautiful young horse of mine? O no; it's out of the question. Who's going to take the washing home to my customers every week? Besides, I'm too fond of him, and he simply dotes on me."

"Try and love a donkey," suggested the gipsy. "Some people do."

"You don't seem to see," continued Toad, "that this fine horse of mine is a cut above you altogether. He's a blood horse, he is, partly; not the part you see, of course—another part. And he's been a Prize Hackney, too, in his time—that was the time before you knew him, but you can still tell it on him at a glance, if you understand anything about horses. No, it's not to be thought of for a moment. All the same, how much might you be disposed to offer me for this beautiful young horse of mine?"

The gipsy looked the horse over, and then he looked Toad over with equal care, and looked at the horse again. "Shillin' a leg," he said briefly, and turned away, continuing to smoke and try to stare the wide world out of countenance.

"A shilling a leg?" cried Toad. "If you please, I must take a little time to work that out, and see just what it comes to."

He climbed down off his horse, and left it to graze, and sat down by the gipsy, and did sums on his fingers, and at last he said, "A shilling a leg? Why, that comes to exactly four shillings, and no more. O no; I could not think of accepting four shillings for this beautiful young horse of mine."

"Well," said the gipsy, "I'll tell you what I will do. I'll make it five shillings, and that's three-and-sixpence more than the animal's worth. And that's my last word."

Then Toad sat and pondered long and deeply. For he was hungry and quite penniless, and still some way—he knew not how far—from home, and enemies might still be looking for him. To one in such a situation, five shillings may very well appear a large sum of money. On the other hand, it did not seem very much to get for a horse. But then, again, the horse hadn't cost him anything; so whatever he got was all clear profit. At last he said firmly, "Look here, gipsy! I tell you what we will do; and this is *my* last word. You shall hand me over six shillings and sixpence, cash down; and further, in addition thereto, you shall give me as much breakfast as I can possibly eat, at one sitting of course, out of that iron pot of yours that keeps sending forth such delicious and exciting smells. In return, I will make over to you my spirited young horse, with all the beautiful harness and trappings that are on him, freely thrown in. If that's not good enough for you, say so, and I'll be getting on. I know a man near here who's wanted this horse of mine for years."

The gipsy grumbled frightfully, and declared if he did a few more deals of that sort he'd be ruined. But in the end he lugged a dirty canvas bag out of the depths of his trouser pocket, and counted out six shillings and sixpence into Toad's paw. Then he disappeared into the caravan for an instant, and returned with a large iron plate and a knife, fork, and spoon. He tilted up the pot, and a glorious stream of hot rich stew gurgled into the plate. It was, indeed, the most beautiful stew in the world, being made of partridges, and pheasants, and chickens, and hares, and rabbits, and peahens, and guinea-fowls, and one or two other things. Toad took the plate on his lap, almost crying, and stuffed, and stuffed, and stuffed, and kept asking for more, and the gipsy never grudged it him. He thought that he had never eaten so good a breakfast in all his life.

When Toad had taken as much stew on board as he thought he could possibly hold, he got up and said good-bye to the gipsy, and took an affectionate farewell of the horse; and the gipsy, who knew the riverside well, gave him directions which way to go, and he set forth on his travels again in the best possible spirits. He was, indeed, a very different Toad from the animal of an hour ago. The sun was shining brightly, his wet clothes were quite dry again, he had money in his pocket once more, he was nearing home and friends and safety, and, most and best of all, he had had a substantial meal, hot and nourishing, and felt big, and strong, and careless, and self-confident.

As he tramped along gaily, he thought of his adventures and escapes, and how when things seemed at their worst he had always managed to find a way out; and his pride and conceit began to swell within him. "Ho, ho!" he said to himself as he marched along with his chin in the air, "what a clever Toad I am! There is surely no animal equal to me for cleverness in the whole world! My enemies shut me up in prison, encircled by sentries, watched night and day by warders; I walked out through them all, by sheer ability coupled with courage. They pursue me with engines, and policemen, and revolvers; I snap my fingers at them, and vanish, laughing, into space. I am, unfortunately, thrown into a canal by a woman fat of body and very evil-minded. What of it? I swim ashore, I seize her horse, I ride off in triumph, and I sell the horse for a whole pocketful of money and an excellent breakfast! Ho, ho! I am The Toad, the handsome, the popular, the successful Toad!" He got so puffed up with conceit that he made up a song as he walked in praise of himself, and sang it at the top of his voice, though there was no one to hear it but him. It was perhaps the most conceited song that any animal ever composed.

"The world has held great Heroes,
   As history-books have showed;
But never a name to go down to fame
   Compared with that of Toad!

"The clever men at Oxford
   Know all that there is to be knowed.
But they none of them know one half as much
   As intelligent Mr. Toad!

"The animals sat in the Ark and cried,
   Their tears in torrents flowed.
Who was it said, 'There's land ahead'?
   Encouraging Mr. Toad!

"The Army all saluted
    As they marched along the road.
Was it the King? Or Kitchener?
    No. It was Mr. Toad!

"The Queen and her Ladies-in-waiting
    Sat at the window and sewed.
She cried, 'Look! who's that *handsome* man?'
    They answered, 'Mr. Toad.' "

There was a great deal more of the same sort, but too dreadfully conceited to be written down. These are some of the milder verses.

He sang as he walked, and he walked as he sang, and got more inflated every minute. But his pride was shortly to have a severe fall.

After some miles of country lanes he reached the high road, and as he turned into it and glanced along its white length, he saw approaching him a speck that turned into a dot and then into a blob, and then into something very familiar; and a double note of warning, only too well known, fell on his delighted ear.

"This is something like!" said the excited Toad. "This is real life again, this is once more the great world from which I have been missed so long! I will hail them, my brothers of the wheel, and pitch them a yarn, of the sort that has been so successful hitherto; and they will give me a lift, of course, and then I will talk to them some more; and, perhaps, with luck, it may even end in my driving up to Toad Hall in a motor-car! That will be one in the eye for Badger!"

He stepped confidently out into the road to hail the motor-car, which came along at an easy pace, slowing down as it neared the lane; when suddenly he became very pale, his heart turned to water, his knees shook and yielded under him, and he doubled up and collapsed with a sickening pain in his interior. And well he might, the unhappy animal; for the approaching car was the very one he had stolen out of the yard of the Red Lion Hotel on that fatal day when all his troubles began! And the people in it were the very same people he had sat and watched at luncheon in the coffee-room!

He sank down in a shabby, miserable heap in the road, murmuring to himself in his despair, "It's all up! It's all over now! Chains and policemen again! Prison again! Dry bread and water again! O, what a fool I have been! What did I want to go strutting about the country for, singing conceited songs, and hailing people in broad day on the high road, instead of hiding till nightfall and slipping home quietly by back ways! O hapless Toad! O ill-fated animal!"

The terrible motor-car drew slowly nearer and nearer, till at last he heard it stop just short of him. Two gentlemen got out and walked round the trembling heap of crumpled misery lying in the road, and one of them said, "O dear! this is very sad! Here is a poor old thing—a washerwoman apparently—who has fainted in the road! Perhaps she is overcome by the heat, poor creature; or possibly she has not had any food to-day. Let us lift her into the car and take her to the nearest village, where doubtless she has friends."

They tenderly lifted Toad into the motor-car and propped him up with soft cushions, and proceeded on their way.

When Toad heard them talk in so kind and sympathetic a manner, and knew that he was not recognized, his courage began to revive, and he cautiously opened first one eye and then the other.

"Look!" said one of the gentlemen, "she is better already. The fresh air is doing her good. How do you feel now, ma'am?"

"Thank you kindly, sir," said Toad in a feeble voice, "I'm feeling a great deal better!"

"That's right," said the gentleman. "Now keep quite still, and, above all, don't try to talk."

"I won't," said Toad. "I was only thinking, if I might sit on the front seat there, beside the driver, where I could get the fresh air full in my face, I should soon be all right again."

"What a very sensible woman!" said the gentleman. "Of course you shall." So they carefully helped Toad into the front seat beside the driver, and on they went once more.

Toad was almost himself again by now. He sat up, looked about him, and tried to beat down the tremors, the yearnings, the old cravings that rose up and beset him and took possession of him entirely.

"It is fate!" he said to himself. "Why strive? why struggle?" and he turned to the driver at his side.

"Please, sir," he said, "I wish you would kindly let me try and drive the car for a little. I've been watching you carefully, and it looks so easy and so interesting, and I should like to be able to tell my friends that once I had driven a motor-car!"

The driver laughed at the proposal, so heartily that the gentleman inquired what the matter was. When he heard, he said, to Toad's delight, "Bravo, ma'am! I like your spirit. Let her have a try, and look after her. She won't do any harm." Toad eagerly scrambled into the seat vacated by the driver, took the steering-wheel in his hands, listened with affected humility to the instructions given him, and set the car in motion, but very slowly and carefully at first, for he was determined to be prudent.

The gentlemen behind clapped their hands and applauded, and Toad heard them saying, "How well she does it! Fancy a washerwoman driving a car as well as that, the first time!"

Toad went a little faster; then faster still, and faster.

He heard the gentlemen call out warningly, "Be careful, washerwoman!" And this annoyed him, and he began to lose his head.

The driver tried to interfere, but he pinned him down in his seat with one elbow, and put on full speed. The rush of air in his face, the hum of the engine, and the light jump of the car beneath him intoxicated his weak brain. "Washerwoman, indeed!" he shouted recklessly. "Ho! ho! I am the Toad, the motor-car snatcher, the prison-breaker, the Toad who always escapes! Sit still, and you shall know what driving really is, for you are in the hands of the famous, the skillful, the entirely fearless Toad!"

With a cry of horror the whole party rose and flung themselves on him. "Seize him!" they cried, "seize the Toad, the wicked animal who stole our motor-car! Bind him, chain him, drag him to the nearest police-station! Down with the desperate and dangerous Toad!"

Alas! they should have thought, they ought to have been more prudent, they should have remembered to stop the motor-car somehow before playing any pranks of that sort. With a half-turn of the wheel the Toad sent the car crashing through the low hedge that ran along the roadside. One mighty bound, a violent shock, and the wheels of the car were churning up the thick mud of a horse-pond.

Toad found himself flying through the air with the strong upward rush and delicate curve of a swallow. He liked the motion, and was just beginning to wonder whether it would go on until he developed wings and turned into a Toad-bird, when he landed on his back with a thump, in the soft rich grass of a meadow. Sitting up, he could just see the motor-car in the pond, nearly submerged; the gentlemen and the driver, encumbered by their long coats, were floundering helplessly in the water.

He picked himself up rapidly, and set off running across country as hard as he could, scrambling through hedges, jumping ditches, pounding across fields, till he was breathless and weary, and had to settle down into an easy walk. When he had recovered his breath somewhat, and was able to think calmly, he began to giggle, and from giggling he took to laughing, and he laughed till he had to sit down under a hedge. "Ho, ho!" he cried, in ecstasies of self-admiration, "Toad again! Toad, as usual, comes out on top! Who was it got them to give him a lift? Who managed to get on the front seat for the sake of fresh air? Who persuaded them into letting him see if he could drive? Who landed them all in a horse-pond? Who escaped, flying gaily and unscathed through the air, leaving the narrow-minded, grudging, timid excursionists in the mud where they should rightly be? Why, Toad, of course; clever Toad, great Toad, *good* Toad!"

Then he burst into song again, and chanted with uplifted voice—

> "The motor-car went Poop-poop-poop,
>   As it raced along the road.
> Who was it steered it into a pond?
>   Ingenious Mr. Toad!

"O, how clever I am! How clever, how clever, how very clev——"

A slight noise at a distance behind him made him turn his head and look. O horror! O misery! O despair!

About two fields off, a chauffeur in his leather gaiters and two large rural policemen were visible, running towards him as hard as they could go!

Poor Toad sprang to his feet and pelted away again, his heart in his mouth. "O my!" he gasped, as he panted along, "what an *ass* I am! What a *conceited* and heedless ass! Swaggering again! Shouting and singing songs again! Sitting still and gassing again! O my! O my! O my!"

He glanced back, and saw to his dismay that they were gaining on him. On he ran desperately, but kept looking back, and saw that they still gained steadily. He did his best, but he was a fat animal, and his legs were short, and still they gained. He could hear them close behind him now. Ceasing to heed where he was going, he struggled on blindly and wildly, looking back over his shoulder at the now triumphant enemy, when suddenly the earth failed under his feet, he grasped at the air, and splash! he found himself head over ears in deep water, rapid water, water that bore him along with a force he could not contend with; and he knew that in his blind panic he had run straight into the river!

He rose to the surface and tried to grasp the reeds and the rushes that grew along the water's edge close under the bank, but the stream was so strong that it tore them out of his hands. "O my!" gasped poor Toad, "if ever I steal a motor-car again! If ever I sing another conceited song"—then down he went, and came up breathless and spluttering. Presently he saw that he was approaching a big dark hole in the bank, just above his head, and as the stream bore him past he reached up with a paw and caught hold of the edge and held on. Then slowly and with difficulty he drew himself up out of the water, till at last he was able to rest his elbows on the edge of the hole. There he remained for some minutes, puffing and panting, for he was quite exhausted.

As he sighed and blew and stared before him into the dark hole, some bright small thing shone and twinkled in its depths, moving towards him. As it approached, a face grew up gradually around it, and it was a familiar face!

Brown and small, with whiskers.

Grave and round, with neat ears and silky hair.

It was the Water Rat!

ACKNOWLEDGMENTS

All possible care has been taken to trace ownership and secure permission
for each selection in this series. The Great Books Foundation wishes to
thank the following authors, publishers, and representatives for permission
to reprint copyrighted material:

Thunder, Elephant, and Dorobo, from TALES TOLD NEAR A CROCODILE,
by Humphrey Harman. Copyright 1962 by Humphrey Harman.
Reprinted by permission of Century Hutchinson Publishing Group Limited.

The Man with the Wen, from WORLD TALES, by Idries Shah.
Copyright 1979 by Technographia, S. A., and Harcourt Brace Jovanovich,
Inc. Reprinted by permission of Harcourt Brace Jovanovich, Inc.

Ali Baba and the Forty Thieves, from TALES FROM THE ARABIAN NIGHTS,
translated by Charlotte Dixon, edited by Dr. Hedwig Smola. Copyright 1964
by Carl Ueberreuter, Vienna, Austria. Reprinted by permission of
Verlag Carl Ueberreuter.

The Goldfish, from THE LITTLE BOOKROOM, by Eleanor Farjeon.
Copyright 1955 by Eleanor Farjeon; renewed 1983 by Gervase Farjeon and
M. S. H. Jones. Reprinted by permission of Harold Ober Associates, Inc.

Prot and Krot, from THE AMBER MOUNTAIN AND OTHER
FOLK STORIES, by Agnes Szudek. Copyright 1976 by Agnes Szudek.
Reprinted by permission of the author.

The Hemulen Who Loved Silence, from TALES FROM MOOMINVALLEY,
by Tove Jansson. Translation copyright 1963 by Ernest Benn Limited.
Reprinted by permission of A & C Black (Publishers) Limited.

The Dancing Princesses, from TALES TOLD AGAIN, by Walter de la Mare.
Copyright 1927 by Walter de la Mare. Reprinted by permission of
The Literary Trustees of Walter de la Mare and The Society of Authors
as their representative.

Allah Will Provide, from THE SULTAN'S FOOL AND OTHER
NORTH AFRICAN TALES, by Robert Gilstrap and Irene Estabrook.
Published by Holt, Rinehart and Winston, Publishers.

ILLUSTRATION CREDITS

Brock Cole prepared the illustrations for *Prot and Krot* and
Allah Will Provide.

Donna Diamond prepared the illustration for *The Man with the Wen.*

Leo and Diane Dillon prepared the illustrations for *The Goldfish*
and *The Devoted Friend.*

Tom Feelings prepared the illustration for *Thunder, Elephant, and Dorobo.*

Paul Hoffman prepared the illustration for *Beauty and the Beast.*

Tove Jansson's illustrations for *The Hemulen Who Loved Silence* are from
TALES FROM MOOMINVALLEY. Illustrations copyright 1962 by Tove
Jansson. Reprinted by permission of A & C Black (Publishers) Limited.

Arthur Rackham's illustration for *Ali Baba and the Forty Thieves* is from
THE ARTHUR RACKHAM FAIRY BOOK, first published in 1933
by George G. Harrap & Company, Ltd. His illustration for *The Dancing
Princesses* is from SIXTY FAIRY TALES OF THE BROTHERS GRIMM,
published in 1979 by Weathervane Books.

Ernest Shepard's illustrations for *Mr. Toad* and *The Further Adventures
of Toad* are from THE WIND IN THE WILLOWS, by Kenneth Grahame.
Illustrations copyright 1933 by Charles Scribner's Sons; renewed 1961 by
Ernest H. Shepard. Reprinted by permission of Charles Scribner's Sons,
an imprint of Macmillan Publishing Company.

Cover art by Ed Young. Copyright 1992 by Ed Young.

Text and cover design by William Seabright,
William Seabright & Associates.